"Now it is a joyful occasion. My wife and son return home with me. Everything is good. Everything is as it should be."

His wife and son....

His *wife*.

Jill's heart hammered relentlessly and her hand shook as she clutched the flute. Was this why he'd ordered the champagne? "So that is the story we're to tell them?"

"It won't be a story. My family has a disreputable history—a history you've thrown in my face. But my father has worked hard to change the past, and I've continued his fight. We've worked too hard, sacrificed too much, to have Joseph inherit scorn or scandal. No one is to know he was born out of wedlock," Vittorio continued quietly. "He is not to grow up marked by shame.

"The ceremony will take place in the next half-hour, before the baby wakes," he said, looking down at her. "Find something appropriate in your suitcase for the ceremony—something elegant and festive. After all, we'll want good memories to help us remember our special day."

All about the author...
Jane Porter

JANE PORTER grew up on a diet of Harlequin®
romances, reading late at night under the covers so
her mother wouldn't see! She wrote her first book
at age eight, and spent many of her high school and
college years living abroad, immersing herself in
other cultures and continuing to read voraciously.
Now Jane splits her time between rugged Seattle,
Washington, and the beautiful beaches of Hawaii,
with her sexy surfer and three very active sons.
Jane loves to hear from her readers. You can write
to her at PO Box 524, Bellevue, WA 98009, USA. Or
visit her website at www.janeporter.com.

Jane Porter

A DARK SICILIAN SECRET

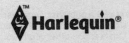

Harlequin®

TORONTO NEW YORK LONDON
AMSTERDAM PARIS SYDNEY HAMBURG
STOCKHOLM ATHENS TOKYO MILAN MADRID
PRAGUE WARSAW BUDAPEST AUCKLAND

Recycling programs
for this product may
not exist in your area.

ISBN-13: 978-0-373-13007-8

A DARK SICILIAN SECRET

First North American Publication 2011

Copyright © 2011 by Jane Porter

A DARK SICILIAN SECRET

For the fabulous Megan Crane
You've been an amazing friend.
I can't imagine my life without you!

CHAPTER ONE

Peace.

Finally.

Jillian Smith drew a deep breath as she walked along the jagged cliff overlooking the stormy Pacific Ocean, relishing the fresh air, stunning scenery and a rare moment of freedom. Things were definitely looking up.

She hadn't seen Vittorio's men in over nine months and she was certain that if she was careful, they'd never find her here, in this small, private coastal town just a few miles outside Carmel, California.

For one, she didn't use her name, Jillian Smith, anymore. She had a new identity, April Holliday, and a new look— blonde, tan, as if she were a California native instead of a striking brunette from Detroit. Not that Vitt knew she was from Detroit.

Nor could he know. It was imperative she keep Vittorio, the father of her baby, as far away from her as possible.

He was so dangerous. Such a threat. To her. To Joe. To everything she held dear. She'd loved him, had come so close to imagining a future with him, only to discover that he wasn't a hero...wasn't a knight in shining armor but a man like her father. A man who'd made his fortune in organized crime.

Jillian drew a short breath, aware of the tension balling in her shoulders. Relax, she told herself. There's no reason to be afraid. The danger's behind you now. Vitt doesn't know where you are. He can't take the baby from you. You're safe. Everything's good.

She paused along the cliff to stare out at the dark blue water crested with foam. The waves were big today and they crashed against the dark rocks below with power and passion. The sea seemed angry, almost inconsolable, and for a moment she felt the same way.

She'd loved Vitt. And maybe they'd been together only two weeks, but in those two weeks she'd imagined a life with him. Imagined so many possibilities for them.

But then the truth emerged. He wasn't a hero—no prince on a white stallion—but a terrifying villain.

The first raindrops began to fall and she pushed back her long blond hair from her face, determined to put the past behind her and focus on the present as well as Joe's future. And Joe would have a great future. She'd make sure he had everything she'd never known—stability, security, a happy home.

Already she'd found a darling rental house just a quarter mile down the road on a quiet cul-de-sac. She'd gotten an amazing job at the Highlands Inn, one of the premier hotels on the Northern California coast, assisting with their marketing and sales. And best of all, she'd found excellent child care so she could work. In fact, lovely Hannah was with Joe now.

The rain pelted down, and the brisk wind whipped at her hair, tugging at her black fisherman's sweater, but she welcomed the fierce weather, and loved its intensity. She couldn't help smiling at the ocean, and the endless horizon, imagining life's possibilities.

"Thinking of jumping, Jill?" A deep male voice spoke behind her.

Her smile vanished as she stiffened in shock, recognizing the smooth, accented voice immediately.

Vittorio.

She hadn't heard his voice in nearly a year, but Vitt's was impossible to forget. Deep and calm, his voice was pitched to dominate life—whether it be man or nature—and it did.

He did.

But then, Vittorio Marcello d'Severano was a force of nature, a human being that inspired awe or fear in virtually everyone.

"There are solutions," he added softly, so softly that Jillian shuddered, and took a nervous step away from him, putting her closer to the cliff's edge. Her unsteady footstep sent loose rocks tumbling from the craggy point to the cove below. The falling rocks sounded like her heart shattering and Jill's throat squeezed closed.

Just when she'd felt secure.

Just when she'd thought they were safe.

Unbelievable. Impossible.

"None that I would find acceptable," she answered flatly, turning slightly but avoiding looking him in the face. She knew better than to look at Vitt closely, much less meet his gaze. Vittorio was a magician, a virtual snake charmer. He could get anyone to do anything just by smiling.

He was that handsome.

He was that powerful.

"Is that all you have to say to me after months of cat-and-mouse games?"

The rain fell harder, drenching Jillian's thick knit sweater so that it ran with rivulets of water. "I believe everything has already been said. I can't think of anything I've forgotten," she retorted, her chin tilted in defiance even though her legs shook beneath her. She was torn between fury and terror. Vittorio was just a man, and yet he could, and would, destroy her world given the chance.

And no one would stop him.

"I can. Let me suggest you begin with an apology," he said almost gently. "It would be a start."

Jillian threw back her shoulders and steeled herself against that deep, husky voice of his, forcing her gaze to his throat. What harm could there be in that? And yet it was impossible to look at his throat—strong and bronzed by sun—without seeing the square chin or the broad shoulders encased in charcoal-black.

And even limiting herself to that very narrow region, her stomach plummeted. Because Vittorio was still everything that overwhelmed her. Impossibly physical and primal, he was the true alpha male. No one was stronger. No one more powerful. She'd tumbled into his bed within hours of meeting him and she'd never done that before. For God's sake, she'd never even come close to making love before but something about Vitt made her drop her guard. With him, she felt safe. Near him, she'd felt secure.

"If anyone ought to apologize, it should be you."

"Me?"

"You misrepresented yourself, Vittorio—"

"Never."

"—and you've hunted me like an animal for the past eleven months," she said, her voice hard, her tone clipped. She would not fall to her knees. She would not beg. She would fight him to the bitter end.

He shrugged. "You chose to run. You had my son. What else did you expect me to do?"

"It must thrill you to have such power over helpless women and children!" she flashed, raising her voice to be heard over the wind and the great angry walls of water crashing onto the beach below.

"You're far from helpless, Jill. You're one of the strongest, shrewdest women I've ever met, with the skills of a professional con artist."

"I'm not a con artist."

"Then why the alias of April Holliday? And how did you manage to create such a persona? It takes money and connections to pull off what you nearly pulled off—"

"*Nearly.* That is the key word, isn't it?"

He shrugged again. "That's for another discussion. Right now I'd like to get out of the rain—"

"You're free to go."

"I'm going nowhere without you. And I don't like you standing so close to the edge of the cliff. Come away. You worry me," he said, extending a hand to her.

She ignored his hand, and glanced up instead, her gaze taking in the long, lean jaw, the angled cheekbone, the very sensual lips above his firm chin, and all it took was that one glance for her to go hot, then cold, and hot all over again.

"And you terrify me," she answered bitterly, looking swiftly away, knowing that his lips had kissed her everywhere, exploring her body with mind-blowing detail. He'd brought her to her first orgasm with his mouth and tongue and she'd been mortified when she'd screamed as she came. She hadn't imagined pleasure so intense or sensation so strong. She'd never known anything could shatter her control. But then, she hadn't ever imagined a man like Vittorio.

But the truth was, she wasn't terrified of him. She was terrified of herself when around him. Because in Bellagio, Vittorio undid her. With just one look, he weakened her resolve. One kiss, and he shattered her independence. From the first time they'd made love, she wanted him far too much, realizing she needed him more than she'd ever needed anyone.

"You're ridiculous," he chided, his tone exasperated. "Have I ever hurt you, or laid a hand on you—other than to pleasure you?"

She closed her eyes as her legs wobbled beneath her. During their two weeks together, two incredible weeks, he had only shown her kindness, and tenderness, and passion. Yes, he'd had his secrets. He'd been mysterious. But she'd ignored her concerns and followed her heart. "No."

"But you ran. And worse, you've kept my only child, my son, from me. How is that fair?"

She couldn't answer because already his voice was doing that strange seduction, where he peeled away her rigid control, stripping away her defenses. He'd done it that very first day she'd met him in the hotel lobby in Istanbul. One introduction, one brief conversation, one invitation to dinner and then she lost her head completely. Took leave from her job. Moved into his villa at Lake Como. Imagined she was in love…something Jillian didn't even believe in. Romantic love was silly and foolish and destructive. Romantic love was for other people, people who didn't know better. She'd thought she knew better.

But then came Vitt, and there went sanity, reason, self-preservation.

Oh, he was too dangerous for words.

He'd destroy her. And Joe.

But no, she wouldn't let him have Joe. Wouldn't let Vitt turn Joe into a man like him.

"He's not Sicilian, Vittorio. He's American. And a baby and my son."

"I've indulged you this past year, given you time alone together, but now it's my turn—"

"No!" Jillian pressed her nails into her palms, barely maintaining control. "You can't have him, you can't."

She swayed on the lip of the cliff, aware that the rain was making the soil a soggy, unstable mess, but she'd never go to Vittorio, nor would she give in to him. Far better to tumble backward into space than let Vittorio have Joe. Because at least Joe was safe with Hannah. Hannah knew if anything happened to Jillian, she was to take Joe to Cynthia, her college roommate in Bellevue, Washington. Cynthia had agreed to be Joe's guardian should the need arise and Jillian had formal papers drawn, clearing the way for adoption. Because it was Jillian's fervent wish that Joe be raised by a loving family. A normal family. A family with no ties to organized crime.

A family unlike her own.

A family unlike Vittorio's.

"Jill, give me your hand now. That ledge could give way any moment."

"I don't care. Not if it means I can protect my son."

"Protect him from whom, *cara*? Protect him from what?"

The concerned note in his voice drew tears to her eyes and her heart lurched within her chest. It took all of her strength to harden herself against him. He'd fooled her once, but she wouldn't be fooled again. She was smarter. She was older. And she was a mother now. Jillian wouldn't be swayed by warmth or tenderness, seduction or pleasure. This was about Joe, and only about Joe. His safety. His survival. His future.

This could have been avoided if she'd only known who she was dealing with when she accepted Vitt's dinner invitation twenty months ago.

If she'd only understood the implications of that date.

But she hadn't. Instead she'd cast Vittorio as Prince Charming and put him on a white horse and believed he was going to save her. Or at the very least, take her to an extravagant, romantic dinner and make her feel like a princess for a night.

The extravagant dinner turned into a fantasy romance. He made her feel so beautiful and desirable that she tumbled eagerly into his bed. He hadn't disappointed. He'd been an incredible lover and even now she could remember how his body had felt against hers.

She remembered the warm satin of his skin stretched over dense, sinewy muscle. Remembered his lean narrow hips and the black crisp hair low on his belly. Remembered the sensation of him extending her arms and holding her still as he slowly thrust into her and then even more slowly withdrew.

He knew how to use his body. He knew a woman's body. He'd quickly mastered hers.

For two blissful weeks she'd imagined she was falling in love with him, and fantasized about living with him, making a life with him, making a home. Yes, there were moments Vittorio was called away to take calls at strange hours, but she'd discounted those calls, telling herself it was just business, or the time difference, and that he was a CEO of a large international company so he had to work at all hours of the day.

He'd told her about his company, too, and she was fascinated by his newest acquisition—the purchase of three venerable, five-star hotels in Eastern Europe—and she'd fantasized about leaving her hotel job in Turkey and going to work for Vitt, helping him overhaul his newest hotels. After all, hotel management was her area of expertise, and she imagined them traveling the world together, exploring, working, making love.

And then on day fourteen, one of Vitt's young housemaids shattered her illusions with the whispered question, "You're not afraid of the *Mafioso*?"

Mafioso.

The word chilled Jillian's blood.

"Who?" Jill asked, striving to sound casual as the maid's eyes darted toward the bathroom door where Vittorio was showering. The maid was only there to bring fresh towels but apparently her curiosity had got the best of her.

"Your man," the maid answered, handing off the stack of plush white towels. "Signor d'Severano."

"He isn't—"

"*Sì*. Everyone knows." And then the maid disappeared, hurrying away like a frightened field mouse.

And then the pieces fell into place. Of course. It all added up. Why hadn't she seen it before? Vittorio's immense wealth. His lavish lifestyle. His strange, secretive phone calls.

Jillian had wanted to throw up. Instead she used her phone to do a quick internet search while Vittorio dressed and the d'Severano name pulled up pages and pages of links and stories and photos.

The maid had been right. Vittorio d'Severano, of Catania, Sicily, was a very famous man. Famous, for all the wrong reasons.

Jillian ran away that very afternoon, taking just her passport and purse and leaving everything else behind. Clothes, shoes, coats—they could all be replaced. But freedom? Safety? Sanity? Those could not.

Jillian gave up everything that day. She gave notice at the hotel, gave up her apartment, left Europe and all her friends, vanishing as if she'd never existed.

She knew how to do that, too. It was something she'd learned at twelve when her family was taken into the American government's Witness Protection Program. Since twelve she'd been an imposter of her former self.

Jillian became Heather Purcell in Banff, Canada, and worked for four months as a hotel operator at the Fairmont Hotel at Lake Louise in the Canadian Rockies. It was there in Alberta, Canada that she'd discovered she was pregnant.

"You had to know I'd eventually catch you," he added kindly. "You had to know I'd win."

Trapped. The word rushed at her, just as the relentless waves crashed onto the sand. But she wasn't a quitter. She was a fighter. And she wouldn't give up. She'd learned through hard experience to be tough, and had been fighting like mad ever since she discovered she was pregnant to protect her child from a life that would destroy him, because Jillian knew that life. Jillian's father had once lived that life, dragging them all into hell with him.

The rain fell harder, slashes of cold wind and water that drenched, chilling her to the bone, but Vitt looked sleek and polished and unperturbed. But then, Vitt always looked sleek, and polished, and unperturbed. It's what had drawn her to him in the beginning. That and his beautiful face.

"But you haven't won," she said from between chattering teeth. "Because you don't have him, and you can torture me, or kill me, or whatever it is you do to people, but I won't ever tell you where he is—"

"Why would I ever want to hurt you? You're the mother of my son, my only child, and therefore precious to me."

"I know what I am to you. Dispensable. You made that more than clear eleven months ago when you sent your thugs after me."

"My men are hardly thugs, and you've turned me into an adversary, *cara*, by keeping my son from me." Vittorio's voice momentarily hardened to match the set of his lean, hard jaw before easing again. "But I'm willing to put aside our differences for our son's sake. So, please, come. I don't like you standing so close to the edge. It's not safe."

"And you are?"

His dark gaze raked the cliff and her shivering, rain-soaked figure. "I suppose it depends on your definition. But I'm not interested in semantics. It's time to get out of the cold." And with a decisive step toward her, he shot out his hand, reaching for hers.

But Jillian couldn't, wouldn't, let him touch her. Not now, not ever again. She leaned away, pulling back so violently that she lost her footing, crying out as she fell. Vittorio, blessed with quick reflexes, grabbed her wrist and held on tight.

For a split second she dangled in midair, nothing beneath

her but the beach and crashing waves, and then her fingers wrapped around his wrist and she squeezed tight.

He could save her.

He would, too.

Vitt hauled her back up from over the edge, pulling her onto her feet and into his arms.

She shuddered as her body came into contact with his. Even wet, he was big and solid and overwhelming. So very overwhelming and she collapsed against him, needing, *craving* warmth and security and safety.

His arm wrapped around her tightly, holding her firmly against him. He felt good. Warm. Real.

For a moment she imagined he might still possibly have feelings for her. For a moment she imagined that maybe they could find a way to raise Joe together, and then reality crashed into her.

Was she mad? Had she lost her senses completely?

There was no way they could be together, no way to raise Joe together. She could not allow Joe to be drawn into the d'Severano world, and yet as Vittorio's oldest son, it's what would be expected of him. And expected of Vitt.

Anguish and heartbreak beat at her. "I can't do this, Vitt," she choked, as he wrapped an arm around her waist, holding her steady against him. "I won't be part of your life. I can't."

He slid his palm across her cheek, pushing heavy blond hair back from her cold face. His hand was warm, so warm, and the caress sent a shiver through her.

"And what is so wrong about my life?" he asked, his voice pitched low.

For a moment she could think of nothing. What could be wrong when Vitt held her so securely? How could feeling good be bad?

Her cheek tingled from his touch and her insides did crazy

flips. She struggled to put together a coherent sentence. "You know," she whispered, thinking of her father, his ties to the Detroit mob and the terrible consequences for all of them, although no one had paid more dearly than her sister.

"Explain it to me."

"I can't." She trembled against him, acutely aware of every place his body pressed against hers. His chest against her breasts. His hips tight against her pelvis. His thighs against her thighs. The contact was both exquisite and excruciating. Her body loved it, him. Her body wanted so much more. Her mind, though, revolted.

"Why not?" He stroked her hair over her shoulders into smooth wet waves down her back.

She drew back to look into his eyes. It was a mistake, as her heart turned over. He was beautiful. Beyond beautiful. But also so very lethal. He could destroy her with the blink of his eyes and no one would stop him. "You know who you are," she whispered. "You know what you do."

The edge of his full sensual mouth lifted, and he tucked a tendril of hair behind her ear, his fingertips lingering a moment against the back of the sensitive lobe. "It appears that you've tried and convicted me without giving me an opportunity to prove my innocence, because I am innocent, *cara*. I am not the man you imagine me to be."

"You deny you are Vittorio d'Severano? Head of the d'Severano family of Catania, Sicily?"

"Of course I do not deny my family or my heritage. I love my family and am responsible for my family. But how is being a d'Severano a crime?"

She held his gaze. "The d'Severano family fills pages and pages of history books. Blackmail, extortion, racketeering... and those are the misdemeanors."

"Every family has a skeleton in the closet—"

"Yours has at least a hundred!"

His dark eyes glittered, the brown irises flecked with gold. "Do not disparage my family. I have nothing but respect for my family. And yes, we are a very old Sicilian family. We can even trace our ancestors back a thousand years. Something I don't think you can do, Jill Smith."

She winced at the way he said her name. He made her feel common and cheap. But wasn't that his point? He was Vittorio d'Severano and she was no one.

He was right, of course. She was insignificant, and she had no one she could turn to, no one strong enough, powerful enough to protect her, because who would fight the mafia for her? Who would take on Vittorio, when not even the American and Italian government could bring him down?

But even knowing the odds, she still had to fight, because what were her options? Let Vittorio take Joe from her? Never. Not in a million years.

Which brought her to her senses. What was she doing in his arms, her body taut against his? It was insanity, that's what it was, and she fought to regain control. Jillian struggled against his chest. "You forget yourself," she gritted. "This is America, not Sicily and I do not belong to you. Let go."

He released her and she took a step away, and then another, walking blindly in the downpour in the opposite direction of her house because she'd never lead Vitt there. Never in a million years.

"Where are you going?" he called after her.

"Continuing with my walk. Need the exercise."

"I'll join you."

"Please don't."

But he followed her anyway, although at a more leisurely pace.

Gut churning, mind whirling, Jillian splashed through puddles as she walked, trying to figure out how to lose Vitt, how to keep him from discovering Joe's whereabouts.

She hadn't brought her cell phone with her, so she couldn't call Hannah and warn her. She hadn't brought money, either, so it wasn't as if she could catch a cab from town.

And so she just kept walking, and the rain kept coming, and Vitt continued following.

"How far are you planning on going, Jill?" he asked her, as they approached an intersection and the pathway turned into a sidewalk with a four-way stoplight.

"Until I'm tired," she answered, worried that the light remained red while his limousine purred just feet away.

The limousine continued to the corner and made a partial turn, blocking the intersection. Blocking her access to the crosswalk. Suddenly the doors of the black limousine opened and two of Vitt's bodyguards emerged.

In any other situation she might have laughed. Who but Vitt would have bodyguards that dressed like Italian fashion models? His men wore elegant suits, exquisite leather shoes and belts, and shaded their eyes with the latest in designer stylish sunglasses. They were sophisticated and well groomed and didn't blend in. They had never blended in. But Vittorio had to know that. Vittorio Marcello d'Severano left nothing to chance.

The bodyguards watched her with professional interest. They were clearly waiting for a signal from Vitt, a signal he had yet to give.

"Tell them to move," Jillian said, turning to look at Vitt.

"But I just told them to stop there."

"Yes, but I can't cross the street with them blocking the way."

"I know. But we can't just walk all day. We have things we have to discuss. Decisions that must be made."

"Such as?"

"How we're going to manage joint custody of our son—"

"We're not. He's mine."

"And which country he'll attend school in."

"The States. He's American."

"As well as Sicilian," Vitt countered softly. "As well as half mine. You can not legally keep him from me."

"Nor can you legally take him from me."

"Which I wouldn't do." He patted his chest. "Fortunately, I have excellent legal counsel, and have spent the past few months working with the best American and Sicilian attorneys. Everything's been handled. I've taken care of the paperwork. The documentation is here. You've had him the first eleven months of his life. I'm entitled to the next."

"What?"

He nodded. "We're to share him equally, or, *cara*, darling, you risk losing him completely."

"Never!"

"You'll be found an unfit mother should you try to run off with him again. And you don't want to be found in contempt of the court. It would seriously damage your chances of ever getting custody back."

Jillian stared at Vitt in horror. "You're making that up."

"I'd never lie to you. And I never have. If we step into the car, I'll show you the paperwork where it's dry."

He made it sound so simple. Just step into his car...just look at the papers...

He must think she'd forgotten just how powerful he was. He must think she didn't remember how seductive and attractive she'd found him.

If she took that one small step, climbed into his car, she feared she'd never be safe—or sane—again.

Jillian swallowed hard, her senses already overloaded. Tall and broad-shouldered, Vitt was undeniably attractive, but twenty months ago she'd fallen for more than his body. She'd loved his mind. He was brilliant. Probably the most intelligent man she'd ever met and she'd enjoyed talking to him more than she'd enjoyed talking to anyone.

Vitt could discuss politics and economics, history and culture, arts and sciences. He'd traveled extensively and obviously had loads of money, but he'd played no games. He'd been warm, sensual—and except for the odd strange phone call, and the sudden secret meetings—he'd been totally available.

And like a love-starved puppy, she'd lapped it all up, soaking it in.

Seeing him again reminded her of just how much she'd liked him and wanted him.

Seeing him again made her realize she'd never be immune to him. "I don't trust you," she said, her voice husky with emotion.

"The problem in a nutshell."

"Don't mock me."

"I'm not. But your lack of trust has created terrible problems for both of us."

She looked away, bit her lip hard, so hard it drew blood. "I want to see the paperwork, but I won't get into your car," she said steeling herself, suppressing all emotion. "Don't try to make me."

Vittorio was still walking toward her and he slid his hands into his black coat's pockets. "I didn't want it this way, *cara*. I didn't want it hard on you." He was just a foot away now and she scrambled to the side. He moved past her, heading to the open limousine door. "But if you insist," he added with an eloquent shrug, "then so be it. We'll do it this way."

Vittorio ducked his head and slid into the backseat of the car with its tinted windows. Jillian watched as one of the bodyguards climbed into the car and then the other. Vitt's men weren't coming for her after all. They were going to leave her alone.

She should have felt relief. Instead she felt fear and dread claw at her throat.

Something was wrong, very, very wrong, because Vittorio would never give up, which meant, if he was leaving her here, and letting her go, he'd already won.

He had Joe. He'd found her son.

Stomach heaving, she rushed toward the car, throwing herself at the door to prevent it from closing. "What have you done?"

Vitt looked at her from the interior of the car. The car's yellow-white light cast hard shadows on his face, making his eyes look almost black and his expression fierce. "It's what you wanted."

"What I want is for my son, my baby, to be with me. That's what I want—"

"No, you had that opportunity and you turned it down. You said you wanted to be left alone. I am leaving you…alone."

Jillian didn't remember moving or launching herself at him, but suddenly she was in the car and the limousine was moving and she was sitting on the black leather seat, next to Vittorio with his two thugs on the seat across from theirs.

"Calm yourself," Vittorio repeated. "Joseph is fine. He's in my safekeeping and with the court's permission, will be flying to Paterno with me tonight."

Jillian's stomach rose and fell and panicked, she searched Vitt's eyes for the truth. "You're bluffing."

"No, *cara*, I'm not bluffing. We had an early lunch together, Joseph and I. He's a delightful little boy, full of charm and intelligence, although I wouldn't put him in yellow again. It doesn't suit him."

For a moment she couldn't breathe. Nor could she think. Everything within her froze, and died a little bit.

She'd dressed Joe in a golden-yellow T-shirt this morning and tiny adorable blue jeans. She'd thought he looked like sunshine and it'd made her smile and kiss his neck where he smelled so sweet. "What have you done with him?"

"Besides treat him to a healthy lunch and ask that he be put down for a nap? Nothing. Should I have?"

"Vittorio." Her voice was hoarse, anguished. "This isn't a game."

"You've made it one, Jillian. You've only yourself to blame."

"What about Hannah?" she asked, referring to her wonderful new sitter, a sitter she'd found two months ago just after she'd rented the house. "Is she with him?"

"She is, but you don't need her anymore. We'll get a proper nanny in Sicily, someone who will help teach Joseph his native language."

"But I like Hannah—"

"As do I. She's been a very good employee. Has done everything I've asked of her."

A cold, sick sensation rushed through her, making her want to throw up. With a trembling hand Jillian wiped the rain from her eyes. "What do you mean, *you've* asked of her?"

Vittorio's mouth curved, which only made his handsome face look harder, fiercer. "She worked for me. But of course you weren't to know that."

CHAPTER TWO

SHE was sitting as far from him as she could on the limousine's black leather seat. Vitt had expected that. She was upset. As well she should be.

He'd just turned her world upside down. As they'd both known he would.

Nothing so far today had surprised him. Jill was the one in shock. Water dripped from her thick sweater and the ends of her hair, and her teeth chattered despite the fact the heater blasted hot air all over them. He found the temperature stifling, but left the heater on high for her, thinking it was the least he could do considering the circumstances.

His limousine had done a U-turn and was approaching the private road off the scenic coastal Highway 1 that led to her cul-de-sac.

Jill's rental house was small, brown, with very 1950s architecture, which meant nondescript. It was a house surrounded by soaring evergreens. A house with a plain asphalt driveway. A house that would draw no attention. Jill was smart, far smarter than he'd given her credit for, but once he understood her, once he understood how her mind worked, it was easy to lead her right into the palm of his hand.

The house.

The nanny.

The job opportunity.

He'd known she was in Monterey County for the past four months, but he didn't want to frighten her away until all his plans were in place. And to help her feel safe, secure, he'd wooed her into complacency by posting the rental house information on a coffee shop bulletin board where she went every day to get her latte. Thirty people called on the house before she finally did. He'd turned thirty people down before Jill made the call, and asked to see the house.

She toured the house with one of his company employees, a lovely woman named Susan who worked for him in his San Francisco commercial real estate office. It was Susan who casually mentioned the job opportunity at the Highlands Inn, an opportunity created for her as he owned the hotel, along with another thirty others spread over the globe.

Jillian had interviewed for the job, and while chatting with the hotel's resource manager, the manager dropped into the conversation that she was just about to let her nanny go as her children were now all of school age, and did Jillian know of anyone looking for excellent, but inexpensive, child care?

Jillian pounced.

The trap had been set.

Jillian was his.

In hindsight, it sounded easy. In truth, it'd been excruciating. He'd wanted to rush in and seize his child, know his child, help raise his son. But he didn't. He waited, fighting his own impatience, knowing that everything he did was watched.

The d'Severano name was a double-edged sword. People knew and feared his family. His grandfather had once been the don of one of the most powerful, influential crime families in the world. His family had been intimately involved with the *Mafioso* for generations. But that was the past. Vittorio's business ventures were all completely legal, and they'd remain legal.

"Shall we go to your house so you can change?" he asked.

"I'm fine."

"But aren't we close?"

"No."

"You don't live near here?"

"No," she repeated, staring out the tinted window toward the street.

He gazed out to the street, too. It was a blur outside the window. Rain drummed down, dancing onto the asphalt. It'd been raining the day he'd met her in Turkey, too. Absolutely pouring outside.

And so instead of taking the car to his next meeting, he lingered in the lobby waiting for the rain to let up. It was while he was waiting Jill crossed the lobby, high heels clicking on the polished marble floor.

He'd known from the moment he saw her across the lobby of the Ciragan Palace Hotel in Istanbul she was beautiful, and she'd shown remarkable intelligence during their first dinner date in the Caviar Bar Russian Restaurant, but he had no idea she could be so resourceful. This woman sitting next to him was street-smart. Savvy. Far savvier than many of the businessmen he regularly dealt with.

"I know your house is close, but if you don't want to go and collect anything…" He allowed his voice to drift off, giving her the opportunity to speak up.

Instead she lifted her chin and her fine, pale jaw tightened. "No."

"Then we can go straight to the airport, and I'll have your house emptied and your possessions packed and stored."

He'd gotten her attention now. Her head snapped around, her eyes blazed at him. "My house is none of your business!" she snapped furiously.

"But it is. Who else would have reduced the rent on an ocean-view home from fifty-six hundred a month to fourteen hundred for a single, unwed mother, with no references or credit, and her young son? I own the house. And you, *cara*, are my tenant."

He saw the moment his words registered, saw it in the widening of her eyes and then the clenching of her jaw.

"*Your* house?" she choked.

He shrugged. "My house. My nanny. My hotel."

"What do you mean, *your* hotel? I've never stayed at an expensive hotel—"

"But you've been employed by one the past sixty days, haven't you?" He smiled faintly. "The Highlands Inn is part of my International Prestige Collection. Or did you not check that on Google?"

Her lips parted. And her brown eyes practically shot daggers. *Brown* eyes. So very interesting. Her eyes had been a dark sapphire-blue some twenty months ago.

"You set me up," she whispered.

"What did you expect? That I'd let you get away with abducting my son?"

"I didn't abduct him. I carried him, gave birth to him, loved him—"

"Good. And now you can love him from the comfort and security of my home in Sicily."

"I will not live in Sicily."

"Fine. You can come and go, and visit us whenever you'd like, but the courts have agreed that based on your erratic behavior, and your inability to provide financially for the child, Joseph will make his permanent home in Paterno with me."

"But I have provided for him! I've always managed—"

"With my help, yes. You forget, *cara*, that the courts are fully aware that I provided you with a home, a job and child care. They understand you couldn't have survived without me."

Her hands balled into fists. "That's not true. I was fine. We were both doing fine!"

"So you say."

She fell back against the seat. "You tricked me."

"I did what I had to do to be with my son."

"And now that you have him?"

"He'll live in Paterno at my family home."

"What about me?"

"You will live with us until he's eighteen and then when he leaves for university, you can go, too. You'll be free to travel, buy a new home, start a new life, but until then, you will live with us in my home."

Jillian dug her nails into her palms. "I'm a prisoner?"

His gaze settled on her pale face, studying the high cheekbones, straight nose, full lips and strong chin. "Absolutely not. You're free to come and go, but Joseph will remain with me, to be raised by me."

"So he's the prisoner?"

"He's an infant, and my son. He needs guidance, and protection."

"From your enemies?"

He regarded her steadily. "I have no enemies."

"Except for me," she said beneath her breath.

"You didn't used to be." He spoke the words just as softly, and her color stormed her face, staining her cheeks a hot pink, a clear indication that she also remembered how responsive she'd been in his bed.

A translucent bead of water fell from a tendril at her brow to her temple. With an impatient swipe of her fingers she knocked the water from her face but not before he noticed how her hand trembled.

She was flustered. Good. She should be. He was furious. Beyond furious. Jillian had hidden her pregnancy, until she had accidentally bumped into one of his employees while taking the baby for a walk. On hearing the news, he'd worked out the dates and rung her immediately. Jillian had the gall to first deny the baby was his, and then when he demanded a DNA test, she ran from him, keeping his son from him for nearly the entire first year of Joseph's life.

Jill should be punished. And there would be consequences.

"In fact, I can still see you at the wheel of my new Ferrari in Bellagio," he added. "You loved driving it, didn't you? But then you loved everything about our time together at the villa in Lake Como. Including spending my money."

"You make it sound like I had a thing for your money."

"Didn't you?" he countered, signaling his driver to move on.

"No!" she answered fiercely, as fresh pink color darkened her cheekbones, highlighting the shape of her delicate face. "Your money meant nothing to me. It still doesn't."

"So you didn't enjoy the private jet, the villa, the servants, the car?"

"Things don't impress me," she threw at him, averting her head once more, giving him a glimpse of her neck and nape.

Her skin was pale, creamy, flawless, and his gaze traveled slowly over her, studying her elegant features and the mass of blond hair that hung in damp loose waves over her shoulders. The blond hair color was something new as well.

"I see. You were there for me." He studied her lazily, as though trying to decide if he liked her better as a glossy chestnut brunette or this California beach-girl blonde, but his lazy, relaxed demeanor was a façade, because on the inside he was wound hard, and tight.

Never in his life had he been played the way she played him. Never. It still astonished him. Jill Smith had seemed so innocent. Sweet. Pure. God, he'd misjudged her. But now he knew, and he'd never be foolish enough to make that mistake again. "You cared for me."

She met his gaze directly, her chin lifting. "I did care for you."

"Past tense."

Her eyes looked enormous but she didn't back down. "Past tense."

He glanced briefly out the window at the twisted, gnarled limbs of a cypress tree before focusing on her. "So what changed, *Jill Smith*?" he asked, emphasizing her name because her name, like the rest of her life, was invented. Jillian Smith didn't exist. Jillian Smith was a fabrication. A very good one, but a fabrication nonetheless.

Her lies had made it difficult to track her down, but he was persistent, and he'd succeeded.

Now all that was left was bending her to his will to ensure his son's health, wealth and happiness.

"Nothing happened."

"No? Nothing happened?" One black eyebrow lifted quizzically.

"No."

"No one whispered in your ear? No one told you something that sent you packing?"

Her jaw dropped a little before she snapped it closed, and yet even then she looked sick. Scared. He wondered if that's what she felt that day in Bellagio when his young housemaid told Jill he was part of the mafia. Silly housemaid to talk of things she knew little about. Silly girl to think he wouldn't find out. His staff had to know there were security cameras everywhere.

"What did you do to her?" Jill whispered hoarsely.

"Fired her." And then he rolled his eyes at Jill's expression. "You think I'd hurt an eighteen-year-old girl for saying the word *Mafioso*? Ridiculous. That just proves how little you know of me. I am not a cruel man. I do not hurt people, or give orders to have people hurt. That's barbaric."

And still she looked at him warily, her emotions volatile as fear, anxiety and uncertainty flitted across her face one after the other. "So you really do mean to take me to Sicily with you?"

"Yes," he answered decisively.

"And you won't keep me from Joe?"

"Not as long as you cooperate."

A tiny pulse jumped at the base of her throat. "What does that mean?"

"It means you'll cooperate. You'll do what I ask you to do cheerfully, pleasantly and immediately."

Apparently she didn't like the sound of that as her brown eyes shot daggers at him. "And if I don't?"

"You will be sent packing."

"You can't do that."

"No?" His dark gaze met hers and held for long, tense seconds. "You will be living in my home, in my country, among my family and my people. Who will stop me? Hmm?"

She inhaled sharply. "You can't use Joe as a weapon against me," she whispered, her voice failing her.

"But isn't that what you did to me?"

"I was trying to protect him—"

"From me, yes, I figured that out. But Jill, what a serious, terrible, tactical error."

Her gaze searched his, a deep line of worry between her eyebrows. "And if I *cooperate* for seventeen years?"

"You'll remain with us, enjoy my protection, wealth and all the privileges of being part of the d'Severano family."

"And yet if I stand by and *cooperate*, you'll succeed at turning him into one of you."

"You make us sound like a horde of vampires."

"You're not much different, are you?"

"According to today's popular culture, vampires are in."

"Not with me."

"You're anti vampire?"

"I'm anti bullies, thugs and thieves. I'm anti predators. Anti organized crime. Anti anyone who forces other people to their knees."

"*È gran pazzia lu cuntrastari cu du nun pô vinciri nè appattari,*" he quoted, then translated the Sicilian proverb for her benefit, "It's insane to oppose when you can neither win nor compromise." The corner of his mouth quirked. "You're either shockingly brave or stupid, Jill, considering you have so much at stake."

"A great deal is at stake. We're talking about the life of a little boy. What we do now will impact him forever."

"Exactly so."

"Which is why I can't just roll over, Vittorio, and pretend that who you are, and what you do, is good. Your values and morals aren't mine—"

He'd heard enough, more than enough, actually, and tuning out the rest of her speech, he gestured to one of his men, who then tapped the glass partition, getting the chauffeur's attention. The driver immediately slowed and pulled off the highway onto the rain-lashed shoulder.

"It's a shame that we couldn't come to an understanding, but I suppose it's better now than later," he said calmly, knowing he was just about to destroy what was left of her world. "I did want this to work out. I think we could have made it work. Unfortunately, I can see it's not going to happen. So let's make the break now and be done with it. No point in dragging the pain out." He leaned to the side, opened the back door. "Goodbye, Jill."

Her lips parted with surprise. "What?"

"Your house is just a half mile back. Not far, but certainly not comfortable in the rain. Do be careful. The pavement is undoubtedly slippery."

She crumpled into the seat, her expression one of horror. "Vittorio," she protested, her voice strangled.

She looked hurt and bewildered. Shattered. But of course she'd be dramatic. Everything she said and did was extreme. But he'd had enough of her dishonesty and distortions. He despised lies and he'd worked too damn hard to restore respectability to his family to allow anyone, much less Jill Smith with her questionable morals and secretive past, to dishonor the d'Severano family.

"Jillian, come. Let's be honest. How can we possibly hope to raise our son together when you dislike me so very much? I want him to be safe and loved, not torn between us. But you would hurt him. You've turned me into a monster and you'd try to turn him against me—"

"I wouldn't."

She was grasping at straws and they both knew it.

"You already have. You've lied to me. You've run from me. You've promised to meet me and then you never showed. But then, you never meant to show. It was just a ruse to allow you to escape. With *my* son." He drew a slow breath, suppressing the anger and shame he'd felt when she'd tricked him following Joseph's birth, playing him, manipulating him for months. No one did that and got away with it. No one. Why should she? "Joseph will be one next month and today is the first time I've ever held him. And you call me the monster?"

She flinched, visibly shaken, and her eyes looked enormous in her now ashen face. For a moment he almost felt sorry for her. Almost, but not quite, because she'd hurt him, humiliated him, and made his life a living hell.

His child. *His.* Kept from him. Who did that? What kind of woman did that?

He gestured carelessly, his tone one of boredom. "Do us both a favor, Jill, and step out of the car—"

"Never."

"I'm going straight to the airport," he continued as if she hadn't spoken. "We have a flight plan in place. I don't have time to waste."

She sat very tall on the seat, her slim shoulders square. "I won't get out."

"Jill."

She shook her head. "I won't leave him. I would never leave him."

"And I won't play these games."

"There are no games. I promise."

"You made promises in the past—"

"I was scared."

"And you're not now?" he retorted, mocking her.

Jill's teeth were chattering again and she bundled her arms over her stomach, holding herself tightly as if afraid she'd disintegrate any moment. "Not scared," she said from between her teeth. "Terrified. Please. Please. No games. No trouble. I will cooperate. I will make this work. I will do everything you ask. I swear."

His dark gaze pinned her, held her captive. "I am out of patience, Jill."

"Yes."

His voice dropped even lower. "There will be no second chances. One misstep, one mistake, one small fib, and you're gone. Forever."

She was nodding, frantically nodding, and tears slid from the corners of her eye.

He refused to care. Refused to feel anything for her. She had it coming. Every little bit of hurt, heartbreak and misery. He'd trusted her. Had cared for her. More than he'd cared for any woman in years.

Twenty months ago he'd actually thought she was the one. The only one. The one he'd marry and cherish for the rest of his life. Which was absurd as he wasn't the impulsive kind.

He'd never met any woman he could imagine as his wife, but somehow he'd wanted her.

He'd wanted to love her, protect her, forever.

And then she ran, and lied, and cut his heart to pieces.

"Whatever you want," she choked, "whatever you say."

She was practically begging now, and he'd thought perhaps it would make him feel better. It didn't.

He'd never treated a woman harshly in his life.

He'd never reduced a woman to this. Nor should he have had to.

Vittorio could hardly look at her. Her lower lip trembled and tears shimmered on her cheeks. She made him feel like a savage, like the monster she'd portrayed him to be, but he was no monster. He'd spent his entire life healing wounds inflicted by previous generations. He'd battled to build back his father's company after his father had been tragically injured and the company had been forced to file for bankruptcy. But he battled for his father. He battled for his family. He would prove to the world that the d'Severanos were good people. "I won't take you out of the country by force."

"You're not taking me by force. I'm choosing to go. I'm begging to go. Please, Vitt. Let me travel with my son."

Something snapped inside of him and he reached for her, one hand wrapping around her wrist, while the other slid behind her neck, his palm against her nape, his fingers and thumb shaping her beautiful jaw. "*Our* son," he ground out. "He's not yours. He's ours. We both made him. We made him together in an act of love, not violence, and he is to be raised with love, not violence. Do you understand?"

"Yes."

Brown or blue, her eyes were mesmerizing, brilliant with raw emotion. He'd thought she was everything he'd ever wanted. He'd thought they'd be able to grow old together. "From now on there is no yours or mine," he continued roughly. "There is only ours. There is only one family. And that is the d'Severanos."

She nodded her head jerkily. "Yes."

And then because there was so much sadness in her eyes, he did the only thing he could think of—he kissed her. But it wasn't a tender kiss and it wasn't to comfort. He kissed her fiercely, taking her lips the way he'd now taken control of her life. She'd had her chance. They'd tried it her way. Now it was his.

The hard, punishing kiss didn't ease his anger. If anything, it made him want more. Her mouth was so soft, and her lips quivered beneath the pressure of his. Angling her head back, he ruthlessly parted her mouth, his tongue taking and tasting the sweetness inside.

Jillian shuddered against him, her fingers splayed against his chest and when he caught her tongue in his mouth, sucking on the tip, she whimpered, her back arching, her resistance melting.

He knew the moment she surrendered, felt the yielding of her mouth, the softness in her body. He could have her then and there if he wanted. If they'd been alone, he would have stripped her clothes off her to prove it. Instead he stroked her breast once, just to make her shiver and dance against him, and then he let her go, watching as she tumbled back against the leather seat.

"Airport," he drawled, adjusting the cuffs on his dress shirt. "We're late."

Approaching Monterey's executive airport Jillian felt as though she'd swallowed broken glass. Every breath she drew hurt. Every time she swallowed she wanted to cry.

She'd failed Joe.

Failed to protect him. Failed to save him.

His life would never be the same now, and it was her fault. Her stupidity.

She should have never left him with Hannah today. Should have never trusted Hannah in the first place.

But Hannah had seemed an answer to prayer; perfect in every way. Her résumé showed that she'd been a preschool teacher with a degree in early education and years of experience working with infants and toddlers. Her letters of recommendation said that her family was local and respected. Best of all, Hannah was cheap compared to nannies advertising services in the paper which made Jillian jump at the chance to have Hannah come work for her.

But Hannah's trickery was nothing compared to Jillian's self-disgust. When Vitt kissed her she'd practically melted in his arms.

There were no words to express her self-loathing.

And so her heart ached while her mouth burned, her lips swollen and sensitive.

Nauseated by her behavior, she dug her nails into her palms. Hadn't she learned anything? How could she respond to Vittorio when she now knew the kind of man he was. Her father had been the same, although he'd been affiliated with a Detroit crime family not Sicilian, but her father had been so ambitious. Her father's ambition had destroyed their lives. How could she possibly imagine Vittorio was any different?

She couldn't.

Pulling through the airport's security gate, Jill caught a glimpse of a white-and-burgundy Boeing 737 on the runway. Vitt's jet, she thought, her stomach free-falling. It was the same jet they'd flown from Istanbul to Milan, before taking a helicopter to the Bellagio villa at Lake Como.

Her stomach did another nosedive and she inhaled sharply, fighting hysteria, as the limousine pulled up next to the jet on the tarmac.

Vitt owned a half-dozen planes, including smaller jets, but this was his personal favorite. He liked traveling with his staff and security detail. He'd told her en route to Lake Como that comfort was essential while traveling, thus the jet's staff quarters, two bedrooms, dining room, luxurious living room and snug but gourmet kitchen that could prepare everything from espresso to a five-course meal.

The limo doors opened and Vittorio climbed from the car but didn't wait for her. Instead he walked toward the jet's stairs knowing she had little choice but to follow.

Apprehension filled her as she followed Vittorio's broad back up the jet stairs. What if Joe wasn't here? What if Vitt had been just toying with her? What if, she agonized, moving past the kitchen and dining room to the living room where her heart seized with relief.

There he was. Her baby. Her world.

Joe sat on a quilt on the floor playing with colorful foam blocks. He still wore his sunshine-yellow shirt and tiny blue jeans and was laughing as a dark-haired woman stacked the blocks into a tower for Joe to knock over.

Suddenly he looked up, caught sight of her and smiled. "Mama."

Jillian rushed to him and scooped him up into her arms. He was small and warm and he fit her body perfectly. And just having him in her arms soothed some of the fire inside her chest. She'd felt like she was dying but now, with Joe in her arms, she felt whole.

This child was everything to her. Life, breath, hope, happiness. And even if Vitt didn't believe her, every decision she made was to ensure Joe's safety, security and well-being.

Cuddling him to her chest, she stroked her baby's soft black hair and then his small compact back. For the first time in an hour she could breathe. As long as she was with Joe everything would be okay. She could handle anything, absolutely anything, except losing him.

Aware that the others were watching, Jillian glanced up into Vitt's face. His dark gaze was shuttered, his expression inscrutable, and it struck Jillian that in the last hour everything had radically changed. Joe's life, indeed her life, would never be the same.

As if able to read her thoughts, Vittorio gestured for the young woman to take the baby. Jillian started to protest but Vitt held up a warning finger.

"This isn't the time," he said, his brusque tone allowing no argument. "We're both wet and we need to change so we can depart. And then once we're airborne, we'll discuss what we'll tell our families."

CHAPTER THREE

JILLIAN stood inside the jet's plush, tone-on-tone bedroom, listening to the door close softly behind her, knowing it was but a whisper of sound and yet inside her head it resonated with the force of a prison cell door.

She was in so much trouble. And she'd brought all this trouble down on Joe's head, too.

And now they were en route to Paterno, Sicily, the home of the d'Severano family, and the center of their power.

Everyone in Paterno would be loyal to Vittorio. Everyone in the village would watch her, spy on her and report back to Vittorio.

Inside her head she heard the sound of a key turning, locking.

Trapped. She was trapped. And the worst of it was that Vittorio didn't know who she was, nor could she let him discover the truth.

God only knew what he'd do if he, the head of the most powerful crime family in the world, found out her real name? Her real identity?

He'd destroy her. He'd have to. It was the code. Their law. Her father had betrayed the d'Severano family, and the d'Severano family would demand vengeance. They'd wanted blood. They'd taken her sister Katie's. They'd insist on hers.

But what about Joe? What would happen to him in this power struggle?

Thinking of Joe snapped Jillian out of her fog of misery. She couldn't panic. She had to clear her head. Be smart. And she could be smart. She'd proven before she'd inherited her father's cunning. Now her life depended on staying calm. Remaining focused. But to remain focused, she'd have to control her emotions, something she found next to impossible when she was around Vittorio.

On her feet, Jillian opened her battered black suitcase on the bedroom's sturdy luggage rack. Her clothes had all been meticulously folded when they'd been placed in the suitcase. Who had done that? Who had taken that much time to pack for her? And then she shuddered, not wanting to think of anyone going through her things, touching her clothes, folding her intimate garments. It made her feel exposed. Stripped bare.

But not totally bare, she reminded herself fiercely, peeling off her wet clothes and changing into dry black pants and a soft gray knit top. Vitt knew a lot, but he didn't know everything. He didn't know who she really was, or who her father was, and he wasn't going to find out.

Jillian stared hard at her reflection in the mirror as she dragged a comb through her still-damp hair.

She'd been a redhead until she was twelve and had loved her hair. It'd reached the small of her back and the soft, loose curls had always drawn attention. Her father used to loop the curls around his finger and call her Rapunzel. Her sixth-grade art teacher had said she would have inspired the great Renaissance artists. And her mother cried when the government insisted on cutting her hair off and then dyeing the shorn locks a mousy brown.

She'd cried, too, but in secret. Because losing her hair hurt, but losing herself was worse. And they hadn't just cut her hair off, they'd taken everything else, too.

Her name.

Her home.

Her sense of self.

No longer was she Alessia Giordano, but an invented name. She was a no one and would remain a no one for the rest of her life.

A hand rapped on the outside of the bedroom door. "Have you changed?"

It was Vittorio's deep smooth voice and it sent a shudder of alarm through her. She squeezed the comb hard as she glanced at the closed door. "Yes," she said, forcing herself to speak.

"We take off in two minutes."

So this was all really happening. There would be no government agent breaking down the door to rescue her. There would be no last-minute reprieve.

Jill's hand shook as she set the comb down. "I'm on my way," she answered, and then lifting her chin, she squared her shoulders and stiffened her backbone.

She would do this. She'd been through worse. She could play Vitt's game. As long as Joe was happy and healthy, there was nothing Vitt could throw at her that she couldn't handle.

Leaving the serenity of her bedroom, she entered the luxurious living area. Vitt was already there, standing near a cluster of chairs on the far side of the room.

Vitt looked polished and elegant, dressed in a dark suit and white dress shirt, appearing as if he'd had an hour to shower, shave and dress instead of just minutes. How he did it was beyond her. Perhaps just having a strong, beautiful face made everything easy. She didn't know. She'd never found life easy.

"You look comfortable," he said, taking note of her simple black trousers and plain gray knit top.

She flushed, aware that he was really commenting on her

dowdiness, and self-consciously she tugged the hem of her cotton top lower.

"Mom-wear," she answered huskily, defensively, hating that she suddenly felt ashamed of her appearance, fully conscious that her clothes were old and cheaply made. He'd hit on a sore spot, too, because she was secretly, quietly passionate about fashion. She loved that beautiful well-tailored clothes could make you feel beautiful, too.

"Which is very practical of you," he said soothingly—which was actually far from soothing. "Now please, join me here," he added, gesturing to the tall honey suede chair next to his.

She hesitated for a fraction of a second, her gaze locking with his. His dark eyes stared back at her and after a moment the corners of his mouth lifted. It wasn't a smile. Instead it was a challenge. He'd thrown down the gauntlet earlier and she'd accepted.

"I'd love to," she answered, forcing a smile, and gracefully sliding into the chair covered in the softest, most supple leather she'd ever touched. But then Italy was the design capital of the world; why shouldn't everything Vittorio owned be exquisite?

She felt his inspection as she buckled her seat belt and crossed one leg over the other. She was trying hard to act nonchalant but on the inside her heart hammered like mad and her head suddenly felt woozy. Tall, broad-shouldered and devastatingly attractive, Vittorio seemed to suck all the oxygen from the room, leaving her gasping for air.

He was too strong.

Too physical.

Too imposing.

The fact that he was also one of the most powerful, influential men in the world hardly seemed fair considering all his other gifts.

Her fingers curled into her palms, nails digging into her skin. This was insane. And this charade would surely push her over the edge.

"I've ordered champagne," he said, taking the seat on the left of hers. "We'll have a glass now, and then another to celebrate once we level off."

How cold he was. How cruel. But why shouldn't he celebrate? He'd succeeded in cornering her, trapping her and claiming his son. She peeled her lips back from her teeth in an attempt to smile but the effort actually hurt. Her heart felt like it was breaking. "Haven't had champagne since Bellagio. I suppose we've now come full circle."

"But back then you were a stunning, voluptuous brunette with straight chestnut hair and Elizabeth Taylor's violet-blue eyes. Now you're the quintessential California beach girl. Blonde, lean, tan. An impressive transformation. Quite the master at disguise."

"I'm glad my resourcefulness impressed you," she answered with a tight smile before turning her head to stare out the plane window.

She hadn't wanted to be so resourceful. She'd been a dreamy little girl, sheltered, pampered, protected. Her parents had been wealthy middle-class Americans. She'd attended an exclusive Catholic girls' school. Her Detroit suburb had been lined with old trees and sprawling mansions.

Nothing in her life had prepared her for the revelation that her father wasn't merely a member of an underground organization, but a traitor within the organization. He was despised by all and when he testified against his organization, he put his entire family in danger.

Overnight twelve-year-old Jillian had been torn from her school, her friends, her community.

Jillian had struggled in their new life, with the new identities. The moves were hard. The isolation at times unbearable.

But over the years she'd settled into being these other people, playing the necessary part.

Her younger sister Katie wasn't as skillful. Nor was Katie as disciplined, or focused. Two and a half years ago—just eight months before Jillian met Vitt in Turkey—Katie had fallen in love with a handsome stranger, a grad student at Illinois University, and feeling safe, had revealed who she really was. She ended up paying for that misplaced trust with her life.

Jillian wouldn't make the same mistake. Jillian had learned that there could be no trusting handsome strangers, least of all men with connections to the mob.

Jillian's throat ached, remembering. She'd been devastated by Katie's death. The phone call from her mother giving her the news had been the most horrific phone call of her life. Even now, Jillian still felt shattered.

Jillian had been the big sister. It had been her job to protect Katie.

She hadn't, though.

And now Jillian had Joe, only this time Jillian would not fail. She would do the right thing. She would protect Joe with her life.

"Jill. Your glass."

Jillian jerked her head around to see the flight attendant standing before her with a flute of champagne. Vittorio already had his. Ruthlessly she smothered the memories of Katie and her family, killing the emotion inside her, smashing down the grief. She couldn't change the past. She could only move forward.

Her eyes felt hot and gritty. She blinked hard, blinking away unshed tears as she took the champagne flute. "Thank you."

The flight attendant disappeared, leaving them alone and Vittorio lifted his glass, dark eyes gleaming above high, bronzed cheekbones, the stiff, formal collar of his black suit contrasting the devastating sensuality of his mouth. "I propose a toast."

She lifted her glass, heavy, so heavy at heart, and waited for him to finish the toast.

He let her wait, too, making her hold her glass high, making her wonder what he'd say.

The jet's engines came to life. Jillian tensed, realizing soon they'd be airborne. Soon she'd never be able to escape.

And then smiling without smiling, Vittorio touched his glass to the rim of hers. "To the future," he said, "and our lives together."

Her heart fell, crashing into her ribs. Was he jesting? What kind of life would there be when there was no love, trust or respect between them?

Again her eyes burned, but once more she squashed the pain with a cool, hard smile. "To Joe," she said instead, changing the toast, her voice as brittle as her smile.

"To Joseph," he agreed. "The son we made together."

They drank.

She swallowed, the cold, slightly sweet, slightly tart champagne fizzing and warming all the way down.

She glanced down into her glass, watching tiny bubbles rise to the surface, admiring the champagne's pale gold color against the cut crystal stemware. Champagne in crystal was almost magical. She'd once loved how a glass of fine champagne could make her feel elegant. Beautiful.

She'd confessed that to Vitt, too, and for one week he'd ordered her champagne every night before dinner.

Did he remember? Is that why he'd ordered champagne now?

Her head jerked up and she looked into his eyes. His expression was shuttered. She could see nothing there.

But once, even briefly, there had been something between

them. Once they'd made love to each other as if their hearts had mattered.

"Feel beautiful now?" Vittorio asked lazily, watching her with those dark inscrutable eyes of his.

So he did remember. "Like a princess," she answered.

"And we're living a fairy tale," he replied mockingly.

She looked away, focused on a point across the cabin. How could she not have seen who he was? How could she not have realized that behind his charm and his stunning good looks was a man of stunning power?

"Can I please go get Joe?" she said, fighting to keep her tone neutral. "We're about to take off and I'd be more comfortable flying if he were here with me."

"But he's fine where he is. Maria is taking good care of him."

Jillian drew a deep breath, then slowly exhaled. Had she heard Vitt right? Was he making decisions for her? Was he deciding how and when she was to see her own son?

She fought the wave of nausea rolling through her. "I miss him, Vitt. I haven't spent much time with him today—"

"—because you left him. You regularly left him."

Again her insides lurched. "I had to work."

"You didn't. You could have come to me. I would have supported you, made sure you could have stayed home with him."

The floor vibrated beneath Jillian's feet. "I wanted the best for Joe. I wanted him to have what I didn't—security. Stability—"

"And you think running and hiding and living with false identities is the way to accomplish that?"

"Joe wouldn't have a false identity."

"He already did! You told Hannah that all of his medical records were listed as Michael Holliday. That when you enrolled him in preschool, he'd be called Mike."

Jillian flushed and shifted in her seat. He was right, and it did sound awful when put like that. "It hadn't happened yet," she said softly, uncomfortably. "It was just a thought."

"No. It wasn't just a thought. It was your idea of a good plan."

She flinched, stung by his mocking tone. He didn't understand that to protect Joe she had to think like a survivor. She had to be aware of danger, had to consider all the different possibilities. "Perhaps I've made mistakes," she said huskily, tears roughening her voice, but she wouldn't cry. Not here, not now, not in front of her enemy. "But I only wanted the best for him."

"And now he has it. His mother and father together under one roof. What a lucky little boy."

God, he was awful and hateful, bent on making her suffer. She blinked and ground her jaw together until she knew she had her emotions under control. "So can our lucky boy join us? Can he sit with his mother and father as the plane takes off?"

Vitt studied her pale face and hard, tight jaw for a long moment before reaching out to smooth a pale blond strand of hair back from her face. She shied away from his touch but he didn't comment on it. Instead he smiled at her almost kindly. "Our son is quite comfortable and sleeping soundly in an infant cot in the staff room. Maria will bring him to us when he wakes."

The jet began to move, rolling forward on the tarmac. "Please, Vitt. Please let me have him. I want him. I *need* him with me."

"Even though he's sleeping in his cot?"

She'd had her life ripped apart by her father's deceit. Her only sister had been killed in an accident the police termed "suspicious," yet they'd never brought charges against anyone. Her mother, terrified of further reprisal, had broken off all contact. Jillian's only anchor in life was Joe. He was the reason, and the only reason, she'd been able to survive so many blows. "Yes."

Vittorio studied her for a long, silent moment. "You really wish for me to have him woken up just so you can hold him?"

She heard condescension in his voice. Condescension and disbelief. Because what kind of woman would put her needs before her child's?

"No," she choked, lifting a hand to shield her eyes so he couldn't see her tears. "No. You're right. I don't want to wake him. It is his naptime. He should sleep."

Again Vitt subjected her to his scrutiny. "Sometimes it is difficult to do the right thing, but I have found that difficult or not, doing the right thing is the only real option."

The jet was moving faster now, racing down the runway, picking up speed by the second. Within moments the jet's front wheels left the ground and then the back wheels. They were airborne.

Dark pine trees dotted the ground. The blue of the Pacific Ocean came into view. In less than an hour they'd leave California far behind. In eleven hours they'd be in Sicily, in his world, and Joe, her baby, her child, would be living in Vitt's home.

And if Joe were to live in Vitt's home, where would she live? Would Vittorio keep her nearby, or would he set her up in her own house or apartment, someplace close by but not in his immediate household?

During the two weeks they'd spent together in Bellagio, Vitt had told Jillian a great deal about the twelfth-century Norman castle the d'Severano family called home. His family hadn't always owned the property. Apparently his great-grandfather had purchased the crumbling fortress in the early 1900s and each generation since had spent a fortune restoring sections

at a time. Over half the *castello* still remained uninhabitable
but Vittorio had said that was part of the charm.

Twenty months ago she'd been anxious to see this historic
property. Now it was the last place she wanted to visit.

"My family is old-fashioned," Vitt said, breaking the silence. "And my mother is extremely devout. At first she might
seem cold, and unapproachable, but given time, she will grow
to accept you. But you must give her time. She is slow to
embrace change."

This sounded far from encouraging, Jillian thought, turning
from the view of the deep blue Pacific Ocean to look at him.
"Is she upset with you for having a child out of wedlock?"

"She doesn't know."

Jillian's eyes widened. "What?"

He shook his head. "I haven't told her. Or anyone else in
my family." He saw her expression and shrugged. "There was
no reason to share such news. You were hiding from me. I
didn't have legal access to him yet. But it's a different situation
now."

"And now?"

"Now it is a joyful occasion. My wife and son return home
with me. Everything is good. Everything is as it should be."

His wife and son...

His wife and son...

His *wife*.

Her heart hammered relentlessly and her hand shook as she
clutched the flute. Is this why he'd ordered the champagne?
"So that is the story we're to tell them."

"It won't be a story."

She exhaled in a painful rush. It was both a protest and a
prayer. *"Vittorio."*

"My captain has the authority to marry us in-flight, allowing us to land in Sicily in the morning as husband and
wife."

"That's crazy," she whispered, her fingers clenched so tightly around the flute's fragile stem that the tips had begun to go numb.

"Why is it crazy? We arrive married, stepping off the plane as a family. Joseph is no longer illegitimate. You are my wife. Problem solved."

Problem solved? Problem multiplied.

Her head spun. She was dizzy with the shock of it. Marriage was so serious, so binding, and even more so among the *Mafioso.* Once you were part of the family, there was no way out. At least not alive. "Your family has never heard of me, and then to produce me from thin air, introducing me as your wife, and Joe as your son—?"

"It would be the truth."

"They'll never accept us this way, Vittorio, surely you can see that. Especially your mother. She'll be hurt that you've kept her in the dark, and suspicious as to why you're only introducing us now. She'll have so many questions—why was there no proper courtship or wedding? Why didn't you tell her about the pregnancy or Joe's birth? You're bringing him to Sicily at nearly a year old. You know that won't go over well."

His eyes never strayed from her face, a faint smile playing at the corners of his lips. "And what would you rather me tell her? The truth? That you ran away when my eighteen-year-old maid told you I was a member of the mafia? That you then hid your pregnancy from me, and then kept my son from me after his birth? Would that be better, Jill?"

She stared into his dark eyes with the flecks of amber around the black pupil. He might be smiling but his expression was one of utter resolve. He was not going to relent. "No," she said after a moment.

"So we have to come up with a suitable story, one that compromises our integrity as little as possible, because I don't like lying to family. I don't believe in lying, much less deceiving my father and mother. But I have a son to think of and I would sacrifice everything to ensure his well-being."

And looking at him, at the steely determination in those dark eyes fringed by the thickest, blackest of lashes, she believed him. But she also believed that there was always more than one way to accomplish something. Life was full of possibilities. There were always options, and those needed to be considered. "You don't need to marry me to introduce Joe as your son. He is your son. He will always be your son—"

"Your point being?"

"That it would be easier for both you, and Joe, if you didn't marry me. Introduce me as Joe's mother. Let your mother think the worst…that I'm a floozy, or a gold digger, or whatever. But at least this way she'll be mad at me, rather than at you."

One of his dark eyebrows lifted. "How good of you to martyr yourself on our behalf. It's gratifying to know you do still have feelings for me."

"That's not what I mean."

"What did you mean?"

Jillian flushed. "That she'll be angry."

"Undoubtedly." He shrugged philosophically. "But I am an adult, a man and the head of my family. I do not answer to my mother, and nor should you fear her. As long as you play your part of the doting wife, she'll eventually be happy."

The words *doting wife* echoed loudly in her head. Jillian's throat sealed closed. What else would she be? After all, she was the eldest daughter of a famous Detroit mobster. Why shouldn't she be married to the head of the Sicilian mob?

And then she pictured her sister, followed by an explosion of color. Her sister's blue, blue eyes. The red-and-gold flames of the car burning. The black-and-white ink of the newspaper article covering twenty-one-year-old Katie Smith's death.

At least her sister died quickly.

At least she hadn't seen it coming.

"Surely there are other options we could explore," she said after a moment. "Roles that would require less acting...roles that would be less of a stretch."

"And what role would that be? My son's nanny? My mistress? My what, Jill Smith? Just what role would you now choose to play in life?"

"Joe's mother."

"And you may. Provided you're married to *Joe*'s father."

She cringed at the way he said *Joe*. He meant for her to cringe, too.

"My family has a disreputable history, a history you've thrown in my face. But my father has worked hard to change the past, and I've continued his fight. We've worked too hard, sacrificed too much, to have Joseph inherit scorn or scandal. No one is to know he was born out of wedlock," Vittorio continued quietly. "He is not to grow up marked by shame."

They were still climbing but Vittorio downed what was left of his champagne and ignoring the seat belt sign, rose.

"The ceremony will take place in the next half hour, before the baby wakes," he said, looking down at her. "Find something appropriate in your suitcase for the ceremony, something elegant and festive. Something that could pass for celebratory. I don't expect you to wear white, but silver, gold or cream would be nice. After all, we'll want good memories to help us remember our special day."

CHAPTER FOUR

JILLIAN fumed in her cabin as she confronted her open suit-case. Silver, gold or cream? Something celebratory for their ceremony?

Ha! He was out of his mind. His power had clearly gone to his head. There was no way she was going to dress up in a sparkly party dress for their vows. Because this wasn't a special occasion and she wasn't celebrating.

He was the one insisting on the wedding. He was the one forcing her hand.

Fine. Force her. But she wouldn't meet him dressed up like a shiny doll without a mind of her own.

No, she'd dress for the occasion her way. Which meant she'd find the plainest, drabbest, darkest dress she owned and wear that for their vows. A dull, dowdy black outfit should convey quite nicely how she felt about their nuptials.

Jillian allowed herself the faintest of smiles as she dragged a high-necked black blouse and a long gray skirt from the bottom of her suitcase. Perfect. Gray and black. Perfect colors for mourning.

Thirty minutes later, Vittorio stood in the center of the jet's living room holding Jill's hands as he recited his vows. His chief pilot, the jet's captain, performed the simple service.

Jill, he noted, had dressed as if she was attending a funeral, replacing her gray knit top with a severe high-collared black blouse and the black pants with a long, narrow, charcoal-gray skirt.

She wore the blouse buttoned high on her neck and her pale hair had been pulled back into a low knot at the back of her head. She wore no jewelry or makeup and couldn't have looked more miserable if she'd tried.

But she did go through with the ceremony, speaking her vows in a clear, almost defiant voice, and holding her hand steady so he could slip the ring onto her fourth finger.

And now his captain concluded the service, pronouncing them man and wife.

The captain didn't linger. With his mission accomplished, he returned to the cockpit, leaving Vitt and Jill to celebrate together.

The flight attendant appeared with more champagne, and a silver platter of delicate appetizers. Vittorio ate and drank, but Jill touched nothing. It didn't particularly trouble him. This wasn't a love marriage—it was about duty, commitment and responsibility, as well as restoring honor to his family.

"Jill d'Severano," he said, trying it out as he studied her pallor and her brown eyes that looked far too big for her small face. "Mrs. Vittorio d'Severano."

She lifted her chin, her expression pained. Apparently she wasn't very fond of the name.

"I wish I could say the worst was over," he added thoughtfully, "but tomorrow won't be easy. Nor will the day after that. But in a week's time the shock will wear off and acceptance will begin."

"It's going to take me more than a week to get used to being your wife," she answered tartly.

He laughed. "I was referring to my mother, and how she'll react to you. But I suppose you're right. You must be in shock, too. How were you to know this morning when you woke, that twelve hours later you'd be on a plane to Sicily, married to me?"

Fire flashed in her eyes. "Your empathy is touching."

"My empathy allows me to protect you instead of crushing you. You should be grateful for that."

She opened her mouth to speak but then closed it, shaking her head in silent, seething frustration.

She looked like a nun at a funeral. A nun minus the wimple. She was buttoned and closed and as emotionally distant as possible. But this was his wedding day, too, and he wouldn't let her do this to him, wouldn't have her play victim, all numb and cold, not when she'd created this situation. And not when he'd worked so damn hard to fix it.

"Unbutton your blouse," he told her, aware that his voice was hard, aware that he sounded every bit as cold as she looked. "You have the softness of a dried up old prune."

She held his gaze. "I like prunes."

"I don't."

"I'm sorry."

"If you were, you'd unbutton your blouse a little, smile a little, act like this isn't the worst day of your life."

"When it really is."

"I should have left you on the side of the road when I had the chance!"

"Too late. You brought me along. Married me. We're now husband and wife."

"And wives are to submit to their husbands."

"To believe that, you must also believe that husbands are to submit to the Church. But somehow I doubt you submit to anyone," she retorted, her eyes huge, her jaw tightly clenched.

His temper flared. She was *not* the injured party. She could not be allowed to play the victim, either. He was the one who'd been cheated. He was the one who'd been kept from his son.

"Do it," he ordered brusquely, "just unbutton a couple of buttons or I'll do it myself."

"We're to consummate the marriage here?" she flashed. "Right now?"

"It hadn't been my intention, but if you're eager—"

"Not at all."

"—and desirous of being my obedient, obliging wife—"

"That's the furthest thing from my mind."

"—then you can pleasure me. I appreciate that you are so sensitive to my needs."

She flushed furiously, her pale cheeks flooding with bright crimson color. "You have many needs, if I recall."

He took a step toward her. "And you begged for it every single time."

Undaunted, she took a step toward him. "You flatter yourself."

"No, if you recall, you flattered me. You were amazed at what my body could do and how I could make you feel. You wanted to know if all men were as well endowed as me, and if others could last so long. You were nearly always reverent when you took me into your mouth—"

"I was tired of being a virgin. I wanted knowledge and experience. You gave it to me. But I've been with other men now. I know what others can do, and oh, can they do."

He took another step toward her and once again she moved closer, chin lifted, eyes bright and challenging. She was deliberately provoking him, daring him to lose control. He was getting close to losing control, too, intensely aware of the hot lick of testosterone, and the primitive drive of an animal hunting prey.

"And what can they do?" he murmured, so very aroused.

She held her ground, chin high, eyes bright as she breathed

in and out in short, jerky gasps that made her breasts rise and fall beneath the ugly black blouse. Her cheeks were a vivid pink. "They make me moan and scream," she threw at him.

"Really?"

"Mmm. And the good ones can make me come multiple times."

This was a fine wedding day, wasn't it? "You've really gotten around."

"Why not? I wasn't your woman."

"But you are now." He reached out an arm, and catching her low around her waist, drew her toward him.

And with his body hot, his groin hard, he roughly slipped his finger between the buttons at her breastbone and popped the first button off. "Just as you always will be," he said, moving down a button and popping that one off, too. "So let's dispense with this blouse, shall we?"

Her lips now were nearly as pink as her cheeks. "Why don't you just lift my skirt and get this over with?"

She spit the words at him as if she could shame him.

He wouldn't be shamed though. He remembered how they'd been together. Intense, physical, passionate.

"Why rush our pleasure?" he asked, reaching out to touch one of the loose blond waves that now fell past her shoulders.

She stared him in the eye, her expression disdainful. "You wouldn't know how to pleasure me if you tried."

"Why do you want to provoke me?"

"Not trying to. Just stating facts."

Facts. His lip curled ever so slightly.

Despite everything, she was still determined to play a game with him, something he found both disturbing and intriguing.

She was either incredibly brave or ridiculously foolish. He wasn't a man to toy with. She had to know that. So why dangle her adventures with other men before him? Why throw his so-called inadequacies in his face?

Brave or foolish, she did intrigue him.

She'd intrigued him in Istanbul and then she'd intrigued him in Bellagio and now here she was, cornered on his plane, his ring on her finger, mocking him. Challenging him. Attempting to defy him.

Interesting, so interesting because so few people tried to defy him, much less a slim scrap of woman who didn't even reach his shoulder. Jill Smith was a complete enigma. She was small and fine-boned and yet so very fierce. She had a heart-shaped face, heartbreakingly high cheekbones and fire in her eyes. She flung her head back as if she were a tigress and to draw blood she talked of other men.

Of other men pleasuring her. Of other men making her moan and scream.

He should want to crush her. He should want to teach her a lesson.

But he didn't. Because he also knew that beneath her fire and fury there was terrible sadness.

He'd sensed it that first night they were together and then nearly every night after they'd made love, she would wrap her arms tightly around him and cling tight. Clinging as if her life depended on it.

He held her against him, her cheek pressed to his chest, and he'd stroke her hair again and again until she fell asleep.

Some nights he felt tears on his chest.

Some nights he felt her take a deep shuddering breath.

But always the sadness, and always his aching need to help her. To save her. To protect her.

That's when he knew he loved her. That's when he imagined marrying her.

He'd marry her and give her a new life, a better life. She could start over as a d'Severano with him.

And now she was, his wife but under totally different circumstances. Which intrigued his mind but left his heart cold.

"I see," he said evenly. "This is your idea of foreplay. You want me to talk dirty, manhandle you a bit, before dominating you in bed."

Two spots of pink color bloomed high in her cheeks. "You're crass."

He felt his lips curve in an unfeeling smile. "And you were the one that suggested I lift your skirt and get it over with. Would you prefer I do it here, against the wall, or would you rather I bend you over the armrest and take you from behind? I do remember you enjoyed it on your knees—"

"Did enjoy," she interrupted tightly, "past tense. Because I will never enjoy sex with you now—"

"Stop. Save the protests for someone who might believe them. I know better. You have always been hot and eager in my bed, and even if you've been with a hundred men since, I know you'll be just as hot and eager again."

Her eyes burned. Her cheeks turned crimson. "I couldn't—"

"You could. *Easily.*"

And to prove his point, he cupped her jaw and dropped his head to brush his lips over the warm satin of her cheek and down to the corner of her mouth. His mouth barely touched hers and yet he felt her lower lip quiver, heard her soft inhale. He kissed her again, just as lightly, a kiss that just grazed her lips, a kiss that was fleeting, teasing.

He could tell she was trying to remain rigid, trying to pretend she was indifferent to him and yet he could feel her rapid pulse in the hollow beneath her ear and the sizzling heat of her skin. She wasn't just warm, she was almost feverish to the touch, and her lips, which had been so tightly closed a moment ago, were parted now. She was breathing in those shallow little gasps that he'd always found erotic.

Instead of kissing her again, he reached inside her torn blouse and plucked aside her bra to cup one bare breast. Her skin felt like hot satin and his body, already hard, throbbed.

He strummed the taut nipple, and then rolled it between his fingers. She arched and inhaled and he pulled her against him, grinding his hips to hers so that she could feel the weight and heat of his erection, rubbing the trapped length between her thighs. She shuddered and arched and moaned.

The moan was what drove him out of his mind. That soft kittenlike cry, a mew of bewildered pleasure, severed all rational thought, annihilating control.

He flicked up her skirt, ran a hand up the inside of her thigh, feeling the quiver in her leg as his palm caressed the taut smooth muscle. He ran his hand up, up until it reached the elastic band of her panty.

He felt the damp heat of her before he'd even touched her there. She was hot, wildly hot, and when he stroked his thumb over the outside of the thin cotton fabric, she jerked and shuddered. She was still as sensitive as he remembered. He stroked her again, brushing the tender clit, watching her whimper and squirm.

She wanted him. And he was her husband. And while he hadn't planned on taking her here, now, like this, the primal male in him recognized that he could, and should. Because she was his. Because she now would always be his.

Sliding a finger beneath the elastic, he stroked her without the cotton barrier, and she was slick and silky and warm, so very, very warm.

He plunged his finger into her damp hot core and heard her sigh and felt her muscles tighten around his finger. He remained still, reveling in her tightness, and her softness, but she was impatient and she bucked against him, wanting friction, needing sensation.

He stroked her, once, again and then with two fingers and

still she arched, and still she whimpered, and they both knew it wasn't enough. It would never be enough. Not between them. Theirs was a physical relationship, an intense relationship, one founded on chemistry, desire and possession.

He'd possess her now, and he'd start with his mouth.

The ugly gray skirt had a loose elastic waistband and he tugged it to her feet in one swift motion. Her panties followed, and then he stripped off her shoes. She was half-naked and trembling but she wasn't afraid. He knew her better than that. Jill, his bride, was trembling with need.

Lifting her, he positioned her over the arm of the suede chair and pressed her back down, putting her butt high in the air. She was completely bare down there, something he liked, finding it erotic to have so much skin exposed. He ran a hand over her cheek, toward the cleft and then down to the soft, plump outer lips between her thighs.

She tensed and quivered as he caressed the cleft again, teasing the swollen flesh until she swung her hips in desperation.

He parted her legs wider, kneeled behind her and took the taut aching bud of her clit in his mouth, alternately sucking and licking until she began pleading with him to mount her, take her. He refused. He wanted her to buck and squirm, beg and groan until she shattered against his mouth and he could taste her surrender on his tongue.

"Please, Vitt," she panted, as his hands held her thighs apart and his tongue stroked and jabbed and then sucked and bit. "Please, please."

But he wouldn't fill her, wouldn't please her until he'd pleased himself by making her come this way. And so he licked her, covering her soft, wet, silky skin with his mouth, sucking harder, flicking the tip of his tongue over the delicate ridge until she broke, crying out as she climaxed in wave after wave, her body shuddering helplessly.

He knew he was a barbarian when he freed himself without taking off his slacks, pulling his length instead from his zipper. Fully dressed, he plunged into her hot, wet sheath while she was still shuddering. It was raw and primitive to mount her this way, but his body was hard and tight and about to explode. With his hands on her hips he held her firmly, taking her with deep long thrusts. He groaned at the pleasure, even as he hated himself for being ruthless. In his heart he knew a woman needed more tenderness. In his heart he'd wanted once to love her, not merely possess her, but possess her he did.

He was feeling even more barbaric as he neared his own climax, certain her body was sensitive, and then as he stiffened, the pressure building, she arched back against him, chest jutting, head thrown back as she came again, crying out even louder than she had before.

He came inside of her, emptying his seed into her and it crossed his mind that this was how it'd happened before. There'd been no protection the first time—although they'd used it every other time—but it'd taken just that one time. Perhaps it'd happen again.

Finished, drained, he slowly withdrew from her, his emotions as numb as his body was exhausted. He expected he'd feel something—pleasure, remorse, relief—instead he felt pain.

Pain.

How could that be? And why? Why should he hurt when she'd been the one to wrong him?

Infuriated by the thick dark emotions churning inside of him, emotions so heavy and aching he couldn't even begin to understand, he reached out and slapped one cheek of her round pert ass. "I think I'm going to like the married life."

And then, emotions wild on the inside, he tucked himself back into his trousers, zipped his slacks and walked out, leaving her to pull herself together on her own.

For a moment after he left, Jillian did nothing. Her legs were jelly. Her limbs shook. It was as if a bomb had exploded and she'd been left in the shattered aftermath.

Seconds passed and then she roused herself, forcing herself to move. Biting her lip, Jill straightened and began to gather her clothes strewn across the cabin floor, stepping into her panties, then her skirt before holding the torn blouse closed.

Numb, so numb, she walked quickly to her room, air bottled in her lungs, her throat raw from holding in all the emotion.

But in her room a tear fell, and then another, and she dashed them away with a furious fist.

She hated that she cried, but she cried not out of pain, or helplessness, or despair, but fury.

Fury with herself. Fury with him. Fury that she enjoyed the lovemaking as much as she had. Because she had. So very, very much.

Yet how could that be possible?

How could she allow herself to feel anything with him, much less pleasure?

And God forgive her, it'd been exquisite.

His hands, his tongue, his mouth…she shuddered with pleasure all over again even as her mind railed against her body.

She was weak.

She was pathetic.

And she'd loved it all—the wildness, the rawness, the passion. It'd been primitive and carnal and hot. Very, very hot. She could still feel the heat of his skin on hers, the weight of his body, the pressure of his hands. He'd held her, shaped her, taken her as if she were his to possess, and apparently she was. Because instead of shutting him down, she'd become hotter and wetter, responding to him with a feverish desperation.

Horrible.

For a moment Jillian felt like her father—a traitor. She'd betrayed herself. Her father had betrayed his mob family. And maybe their sins weren't of the same magnitude, but still, the genetic link was there, as well as the same weakness of character.

Her stomach cramped at the thought. She couldn't bear the idea that she was like her father. He'd hurt so many people. He'd destroyed their family. She refused to be like him.

Walking into the small ensuite bath, Jillian let her clothes fall and then stepped into the narrow shower, turning the water on full force. It was cold. She felt icy. But icy and cold was so much better than the last lingering effects of her feverish desire.

Taking the bar of French lavender soap, she scrubbed her skin, washing away Vittorio's scent and imprint, telling herself she was not his, that she did not belong to him even though everything inside her whispered, *you will always want him.*

She feared it was true. Despite everything, there was something about him that connected with her. Something about him that mattered so much to her.

Biting her lip, she rinsed her thighs as she felt the soreness inside, where Vitt had been. He was large and he'd taken her hard and this was the first time she'd had sex since Joe's birth.

But Vittorio didn't know that. Vittorio thought she'd been with dozens of men because that's what she'd told him.

Scalding tears burned the back of her eyes but she wouldn't let them fall. Instead she tipped her head back and let the water course down, drumming strength into her, drumming confidence.

There'd be no more tears.

She needed to be focused and smart and think about what would happen when they reached Sicily.

She was entering Vittorio's world tomorrow morning, arriving in Catania as his wife. That should make her feel protected. Respected.

Unfortunately the rushed ceremony made her feel exactly the opposite. The ceremony did not seem binding. Never mind honorable. Maybe the marriage gave Joe Vittorio's name, but it did nothing to ease her fears, or her sense of isolation.

She was still vulnerable.

In Sicily, she'd need Vittorio's protection.

How to get his protection and his family's respect? It wouldn't be with a quickie wedding, she knew that much. If Vitt's mother was as devout as Vitt said she was, she'd never accept Jillian as her daughter-in-law, not unless she believed their union had been sanctioned by the church. But how could their union be blessed by the church, if they hadn't even married in a church, or by a priest?

Her stomach did another nervous flip as she realized she needed a public acknowledgment that she and Vitt had indeed exchanged vows, and that they viewed their vows as holy and binding.

Which meant they needed a church wedding.

Fast.

Jillian dressed and blew dry her hair with care. She was just putting on earrings when a knock sounded on the door and she opened the door to discover Maria in the hall with Joe.

"Mama," he said, smiling and reaching for her.

What a lovely surprise! Jillian took her baby from Maria and hugged him tight. His small sturdy arms wrapped around her neck and she kissed his neck, his cheek, loving the sweet smell of him. Her baby. Her boy.

"*Signore*, Signor d'Severano has said dinner will be served in fifteen minutes."

"We're dining with Joe?"

Maria shook her head. "I do not think so. I believe it is just you and Signor, although he thought Joseph could join you for the first few minutes."

"Come in, then. I'm almost ready. Just need to finish styling my hair."

In front of the mirror in the bathroom, Jillian gathered her blond hair, shaping and pinning it into a soft French twist before stepping back to examine her reflection. With her fair hair up, and in the soft silver knit top and dark pewter slacks, she could almost pass for elegant. The top and slacks were big on her, items left over from her transition wardrobe following Joe's birth, but with pink lipstick, silver bangles on her wrist and a sophisticated hairstyle, she looked polished. Serene. Strong.

Serene and strong was good, because when she joined Vittorio for dinner, she had a purpose.

She was going to convince Vittorio that they needed to marry again, but this time in a beautiful ceremony in his hometown, in his family's church, in front of his community of family and friends.

She wasn't sure how he'd react to the proposed ceremony. She only knew she had to convince him it was necessary.

Finished dressing, Jillian thanked Maria for taking care of Joe and then carried her son to the dining room. Vittorio joined her almost immediately and she watched as he entered the room in a crisp white dress shirt with dark tailored trousers. His black hair was again damp and neatly combed, his hard, handsome features set.

She should hate him. She should.

She couldn't.

Because just looking at him, she wanted him all over again. Just seeing his beautiful face with that chiseled jaw and full, sensual mouth made her body warm.

Was it only an hour ago he'd parted her legs and covered her most sensitive skin with his lips? She remembered the way he'd sucked and licked and tasted her. It'd been wanton lovemaking. So very carnal. And yet it'd been exquisite, too. Who knew such pleasure was possible?

Yet desire came with a price. And hadn't she learned by now that those who needed others gave up power?

And wasn't she sick of being powerless?

Ever since she was a child, she'd been at the mercy of others. First, her father. Then, the government. Between twelve and twenty they'd lived in five different states with four different identities. Each new identity required a new image, a new name, a new history.

At first it'd been difficult to remember the script. Lee Black of Ashford, Oregon. Carol Cooper from Fountain Hills, Arizona. Anne Johnson, Fredericksburg, Texas. Jillian Smith, Visalia, California.

And then it stopped being hard, because she stopped caring. It was easier not to try to fit in. Easier not to make friends. Why bother to make friends when you'd soon have to leave them without a word of explanation, or the hope of ever seeing them again? In the government's Witness Protection Program there was no such thing as change of address cards, forwarding phone numbers, email exchanges. In the Witness Protection Program you simply vanished into thin air.

That lack of stability, and lack of control, transformed her from the innocent, sheltered little girl she'd been, a girl who'd adored her father, a girl who'd felt so very safe, into the woman she was today.

From the time she'd left home to go to college, she'd had one goal—to be completely independent. She'd gone to graduate school after finishing Gonzaga University to earn a master's degree in hospitality management, an advanced degree in the hotel and tourism industry, thinking it was a practical study, one that would catapult her to the top. Because the one thing she'd always wanted was power of her own. Power to choose. Power to travel. Power to become someone else.

And she'd come so close to having that power and freedom. In Istanbul she'd been delighted by her job, her apartment, her clever circle of friends. But then she'd met Vittorio, and accepted his dinner invitation and her life had never been the same.

She'd given up everything that one night without even knowing it.

"I still can't get over the fact that you're blonde," he said, approaching her.

"It doesn't please you?" she said, shifting Joe in her arms.

"It wasn't done to please me." As he neared her, his dark eyes met hers and held. "It was done to hide from me. It was done to keep him from me," he added, nodding at Joe.

She held her ground, refusing to be intimidated. "True."

"And you're not the least apologetic."

"I did what I thought was necessary," she answered, aware that Joe was watching his father with obvious fascination. "But that's behind us. We must close the door on the past. Now you're my husband. My protector. I have nothing to fear with you at my side."

He looked at her for a long moment. "And you have nothing to fear as long as you are honest with me." His dark eyes burned her with searing intensity. "As long as I can trust you."

And then he held his arms out for his son.

CHAPTER FIVE

As JILLIAN relinquished Joe, her lips curved in a terrible self-mocking smile.

She had nothing to fear as long as she was honest with Vitt.

Which meant she had everything to fear because she could never be honest with him. She could never share her past with him, at least, not until she knew she was safe with him. Not until she knew she could trust him, because she'd be trusting him with her life.

It was that simple, because her secrets were that dangerous.

Look at what had happened to Katie. She'd shared the wrong thing with the wrong person and it'd killed her. Jillian couldn't make the same mistake. Not when Joe needed her so much.

But watching Vittorio hold her son——*their* son——Jillian marveled over the fact that Joe didn't cry or go rigid when Vitt took him from her. If anything Joe looked supremely comfortable, as well as extremely content in Vitt's arms. It was the strangest thing, too, because Joe was never relaxed with strangers, and even less with men, as he'd been around so few in his first year of life. Yet here he was, held securely against Vitt's broad chest, nonchalantly studying his chubby baby hands as if this sort of thing happened every day.

Remarkable.

Extraordinary.

Vittorio and Joseph already fit together. And they certainly looked like they belonged together. Both had the same dark glossy hair, although Joe's was baby-fine, and the same intensity of expression, even though Joe's eyes were blue and Vitt's amber brown.

"You've held babies before," Jillian said, trying to come to terms with her intensely ambivalent emotions. None of this was supposed to have happened. Being here, like this, was her worst fear and yet nothing terrible had happened yet. Maybe nothing terrible would.

"I have four nieces and three nephews and I've held each one within hours of his or her birth," he answered.

The overhead light played off Vitt's sculpted cheekbones, strong nose and angular jaw. On someone else the nose might have been too long, the bridge too broken, but on him it was perfect. Vitt's eyes, shaded by that dark slash of eyebrow, and the curve of his full sensual mouth, were almost too beautiful. He needed a nose of character, and he had one.

"Your brothers and sisters live close then?" she asked, forcing her attention from his arresting face to the conversation. She would soon meet his family, and tomorrow she'd be expected to live amongst them. Who would have thought any of this possible?

Vitt dipped his head, pressed a kiss to Joe's temple. "Two do. The other two are in different countries. But I'm always there when a baby arrives. Nothing is more important than family."

She swallowed hard, hit by a wave of loss. Those were the very same words her father used to say when she was a little girl.

His two favorite expressions had been "There's nothing

more important than family" and "Family is everything." Only he hadn't meant it.

Or maybe once he'd meant it, before he'd become consumed by greed and reckless ambition.

"I agree," she said softly, hating the awful emotions churning inside of her. Growing up she'd been a daddy's girl. He'd adored her and she'd loved him deeply in return. He'd been such a handsome, gregarious father. Outgoing. Charming. Full of jokes and laughter.

And then it all changed, virtually overnight. Her father, learning he'd be arrested and prosecuted for a long laundry list of crimes, cut a deal with the feds and confessed his part, and everyone else's role in organized crime. He saved himself but sold his crime family out.

He should have gone to prison. Because even fourteen years after her father confessed everything to the government, revealing everything he knew, and giving up everyone he'd known, he remained hated and hunted. He'd done the unthinkable. He'd turned on his people, and the mob had turned on him.

"Are you feeling all right?" Vitt asked, shifting Joe in his arms and scrutinizing her face.

She tried to smile but her eyes burned and acid rose up in her throat. Discovering at twelve that the father she'd loved more than life itself, was a thief, a traitor and a coward, had broken her heart. She'd lived with shame every day since. "I'm fine."

"Do you need some mineral water?"

Did she need mineral water? No. She needed forgiveness. She needed peace. She needed grace. And most of all she needed to forget she was Frank Giordano's daughter. But married to Vittorio, she could never forget. Married to Vittorio, she'd never be forgiven. "That sounds like a good idea."

He took a couple steps, pressed a button on the wall and in seconds the flight attendant appeared. "Yes, sir?"

"A mineral water, and some crackers or dry biscuits."

The flight attendant disappeared to fulfill the request and Vitt drew a chair from the table. "Come, Jill, sit, before you faint."

Perhaps if he knew the truth now, perhaps if she confessed everything right away, he'd possibly forgive her. Perhaps he'd even understand…because surely, he wouldn't really hurt her…she couldn't believe he would hurt her, not after their two weeks together in Bellagio….

Katie flashed to mind.

Had Katie thought the same thing about her new boyfriend, Marco, the handsome law student she'd wanted to bring home to meet Mom and Dad? Had Marco made her believe that she was safe? That he could be trusted? Had she opened up and shared everything, thinking she'd finally found someone who would protect her?

Her eyes burned gritty and pain rolled through Jillian, hard, heavy, sharp, obliterating everything but a desperate determination to survive. To survive at all costs. And to make sure her son did, too.

So even if Vittorio wouldn't hurt her, Jillian knew there could be no confessing, no pleading of innocence or begging for protection. Instead she'd play the role she'd agreed to play.

She gave Vittorio a calm, steady look, maintaining the steely façade she'd so carefully cultivated over the past year and a half. "Feeling guilty for treating me so callously earlier?" she asked, taking the offered chair.

He gazed down at her, black eyebrow arching slightly. "You practically wept with pleasure. I'm glad I could still satisfy you."

She crossed her legs, feeling the tenderness between. "Is

this how our relationship is going to be? You take what you want, when you want, and I comply?"

"But of course. You're my wife."

"Yet you make me feel like your whore."

The moment the words left her mouth she knew she'd said the wrong thing. She didn't even need Vittorio to speak to know she'd blundered. The ugly words hung there, suspended, between them.

Did she really feel like a whore?

Or had he merely possessed her the way he knew best—thoroughly and totally?

She opened her mouth to retract the words but was cut short by the appearance of the flight attendant who'd arrived with a small bottle of Perrier, a glass and a plate of crackers balanced on a silver tray. The attendant was pretty and professional and until now had been extremely poised, but her expression faltered as she sensed the mood.

The mood wasn't good.

The mood would be even worse when she left.

The pretty brunette placed the silver tray on the table near Jillian's elbow and then Vittorio transferred Joe into her arms. "Have Maria feed him dinner," he said, giving his son a comforting pat on the back. "Tell Maria we'll be sure to see him before he goes to bed."

And then they were alone again, and in the silence and stillness Jillian felt panic. She'd said too much, perhaps pushed him too far.

With a shaking hand she poured the bubbling water into her short crystal glass. The water tumbled and splashed.

"Whore?" Vittorio repeated softly.

She couldn't speak. She didn't know where to look. The atmosphere weighed heavily on her, thick and tense.

"That's a horrendous thing to say," he said.

She bent her head.

"Do not ever use that word again," he added furiously. "You're my son's mother and my wife and I will not have you demean yourself—or our relationship—in that manner."

Her stomach churned and Jillian swallowed compulsively, fighting the nausea. Relationship? What relationship? There was no relationship. He was the dictator, the emperor, the ruler. She was his prisoner, his captive, his slave. He had utter and complete control and she would be lucky to survive the next week, much less a month with him.

Jillian drew another breath, gulping fresh air into her lungs. "We do not have much of a relationship."

"Then we'll build one."

She averted her head, bit her lip, holding back the hot retort that burned within her.

"We'll start over," he added. "Tonight. Now. Let's begin again."

She looked at him swiftly, and the intensity in his expression burned her. She flashed back to their lovemaking earlier and she shivered at the flood of erotic memories. It'd been so hot between them. Scorching.

She felt scorched all over again by the heat and desire in his dark eyes. Her whole body responded, breasts aching, nipples tightening.

"Easier said than done," she answered huskily, mesmerized by the chemistry between them. That sizzling physical connection was always there, and it'd been that way from the beginning.

He smiled at her, a lazy, sexy, smoldering smile. "Why didn't you wear this to the ceremony?" he asked, reaching out to touch her silver top. "This would have been far more suitable," he added, letting his finger slip down, stroking from her shoulder over one peaked breast.

His finger lingered on the tight, taut nipple.

She inhaled quickly at the sharp stab of sensation between her thighs. "Not for me," she said.

"Why not?"

She took another quick breath. "I was angry. Little girls do not dream of marrying in secret, shameful ceremonies on airplanes."

"Shameful?"

"There were no witnesses. No family. No friends. Our son wasn't even there."

Vitt's hand fell away and his brow furrowed. "The goal wasn't to have a formal wedding, but to join us together. The goal was to protect Joseph and give him my name."

"I understand. But you asked me why I didn't wear something more festive, and I told you. I didn't feel good about our wedding. It didn't feel right."

He studied her for a long moment. "What would have felt better? A church wedding?"

"Yes."

"I didn't think you were religious."

"I was raised Catholic."

"You never told me."

"You never asked."

For a long moment he said nothing. Then he rose and paced the room silently for several minutes. Finally he paused and looked at her. "The vows are binding, regardless of where we said them."

"I understand."

He frowned at her, clearly uncomfortable. "But you were disappointed by our ceremony?"

She licked her lips. "Yes."

"You used the word *shameful.*"

"It just felt that way. It was so…rushed and hush-hush. We don't even have any pictures to show Joe when he's older. And I can't help but think that one day he'll want to know how we met, and what our wedding was like. How will he feel when we've no wedding photographs to show him?"

"That's ridiculous," Vittorio said, moving to the narrow sideboard to pour himself a neat shot of whiskey.

"I know. I'm just being foolish. Not all weddings are music and candles and flowers with your friends and family gathered around. And just because I imagined a certain kind of wedding doesn't mean I needed it. Joe is what's important. Joe should be our only concern—" She broke off as the jet suddenly shuddered in a pocket of turbulence.

Holding her breath, Jillian watched the water slosh wildly in her glass. For several moments the jet bounced, up, down, up, down, and the glass and bottle on the table rattled and danced toward the edge of the table, and then just as abruptly the turbulence ceased.

All was smooth again but Jillian's heart still raced. "I hate turbulence," she whispered, mouth dry.

"It's over."

"I know, but I still hate it."

"But if we didn't have turbulence, we'd never appreciate a smooth flight."

Their dinner was a strange meal, an almost painfully civilized meal, with Vittorio playing the role of attentive host. They discussed only safe topics—their mutual love of Turkey, favorite European cities, the stunning Dalmatian coast as if both were determined to put their best foot forward.

Could they really start fresh? Could they make their relationship work?

"We're not entirely incompatible," he said just moments later, as if he could read the emotions flitting over her face. "We both like sex and apparently still enjoy it together."

She felt as though he'd dashed cold water over her head. "And that's enough for you?"

His dark eyes met hers. "It wouldn't be, but we also have Joseph and we share responsibility for him."

And that was a terribly important responsibility. Jillian couldn't imagine anything else ever being so important. "Yes."

Vitt continued to hold her gaze. "Maybe another ceremony wouldn't be a bad idea. Maybe we should renew our vows at the chapel, and include our families. It would be good to have them on our side."

"They won't be now?"

"No. Not entirely."

"Why not?"

His mouth quirked. "You're not Sicilian."

They left the small elegant dining room for the staff room and found Joe happily playing with a set of toy cars with one of Vitt's bodyguards. Maria watched from an armchair nearby.

Looking at Joe it struck Jillian that in Vitt's world Joe was royalty. He was treated like a young prince. Protected. Pampered. He was the heir to his father's throne.

It was both a terrible truth and a heartbreaking reality. Joe was no longer her baby, her son. He'd already become Joseph d'Severano, inheriting all the power, wealth and control that accompanied the d'Severano name.

They stayed in the staff room for a few minutes and Vittorio talked to his bodyguards as if they were close friends. And maybe they were. Then conversation ended, he swung Joe into his arms and led the way to Jillian's room where the baby's travel cot had been set up.

Her tiny plush bedroom felt absolutely claustrophobic with Vittorio there. She did her best to pretend he wasn't watching every move she made. Acting as natural as possible, Jillian gave Joe a sponge bath and then dressed him in his footed, zippered sleeper for bed.

Vitt half smiled at Joe's bright blue footed pajamas. "Babies all over the world must wear these."

"Snug sleepwear is essential," she answered, fastening the little flap that covered the zipper head. "You don't want a baby to get tangled up or in trouble."

For a moment Vitt was silent, his powerful body still. "Was it hard raising him on your own?"

"Yes." She looked up at him, her expression rueful. "Especially in the beginning. I was so tired. So terribly sleep-deprived."

"Did you have anyone to help you?"

She shook her head. "No."

"Not even your mother?"

"I haven't seen her in years."

Vittorio watched as she expertly juggled Joe on her hip and prepared a bottle. "So there never were any worries? He's given you no fits? No scares?"

"I didn't say that. I worried about him every single night. For the first six months of his life I woke again and again during the night to make sure he was safe, to make sure he was breathing. I was absolutely terrified that when I closed my eyes, something would happen to him."

"You mean like SIDS?"

She nodded. "You probably think that's silly."

"Not at all." He reached out a hand and held it over Joe, as if bestowing a blessing. "One of my cousins lost his son to SIDS. It was devastating."

"I can't imagine anything more horrible," she said, holding Joe closer.

"Neither can I."

Jillian struggled to wrap her mind around such a tragedy. "Did your cousin have other children?"

"A little girl. She was almost three at the time." Vittorio

shook his head. "Christopher lost his life six months later. It was a very hard time in the family."

Jillian shivered at the grim direction their conversation had taken even as Vitt's words stirred a ghost of a memory.

Years ago a young Sicilian immigrant named Christopher had died in Detroit after her father accused him of double-crossing Detroit's crime family. Christopher claimed he was innocent, without any connections to organized crime, but it didn't save him. "How…how did he die?"

"He was shot."

"Where…where did it happen?"

"In the States."

"I know, but *where*?"

Vitt gave her a hard look. "Does it matter?"

She shook her head, but on the inside, she knew it did matter. It mattered too much.

"Were you serious about having us renew our vows in the d'Severano chapel?" she asked, suddenly desperate to change the subject.

"Yes." He suddenly smiled. "Provided you don't wear black again."

She couldn't resist his smile. "I won't. I promise."

"Good." He stood there another moment, tall, broad, imposing, considering her. "I suppose that means we better get you a proper dress."

"No—"

"Yes. If we're going to do this again, we better do it right, which means making sure it's the wedding every girl dreams of."

He left them then, excusing himself to get some work done, and after he'd gone, Jillian gave Joe a bottle and then tucked him into his travel cot.

But after putting Joe to bed, she didn't know what to do with herself. Was she supposed to join Vittorio? Was she supposed to stay here? What did one do when you were married but didn't feel like a wife?

She ended up staying with Joe. After dimming the lights as much as she could, she curled up on the bed to watch him sleep.

Awake, Joe stole her heart. Sleeping, Joe broke it. He looked peaceful and impossibly sweet in his little cot with his arms stretched out above his head. His soft skin was flushed pink and his long eyelashes rested in dark crescents on his round cheeks.

Hard to believe that just a year ago she was pregnant with him. Hard to believe life could change so much in one year. From birth to boy in just eleven months. Impossible. Magical.

Although the early weeks of her pregnancy weren't magical. Those weeks were filled with panic, and denial.

In the beginning, she didn't believe she was pregnant. She didn't feel pregnant. She didn't feel like anything, certainly not as though she was carrying a child, much less Vittorio's child.

There were times she nearly convinced herself that it wasn't so. She hadn't changed her clothes size. She didn't have any cravings. She didn't feel queasy or headachy or emotional. But her period never came, and her breasts grew fuller, heavier, and her flat, taut belly took a gently rounded shape. Finally she went to the doctor and he told her everything she needed to know. She was approximately seventeen weeks, the baby had a strong heartbeat, development looked good, and unless the doctor was mistaken, it appeared to be a boy.

A boy.

Another male d'Severano.

In that moment, lying there in the paper gown, with the ultrasound machine at her side, she vowed her son would never become his father. She vowed her baby would not become her father, either. Her baby, this unborn son, would have a normal life. A happy life. A life as far from organized crime as possible.

For the rest of the pregnancy she felt secure, confident she'd made the right decision.

She felt so confident, she left Banff when she reached her seventh month, returning to the States so that when Joe was born he'd be American.

Jillian settled on Bellingham, Washington, a university town just across the border from Canada. She found a reasonably priced apartment close to Fair Haven, Bellingham's charming historic district filled with coffeehouses, bookstores and antiques shops.

Joe's birth was uncomplicated and she returned to her apartment ready for the next phase of her life.

But then fate intervened.

Just a month after Joe's birth, Jillian was pushing him in his stroller, enjoying the May sunshine when she bumped into a woman she'd worked with in Istanbul. The woman had neither been a friend nor foe, just an acquaintance, but they both exclaimed at the amazing coincidence of meeting like this, so far from Turkey, in the most northwest corner of the United States.

Jillian had initially been alarmed by the meeting but realized the woman knew nothing about her relationship with Vittorio and therefore would have no stories to tell.

Jillian was wrong.

Within a week of bumping into her former colleague, Jillian received the first phone call from Vittorio. He'd heard about the baby. He wanted to know if the baby was his.

She told him no.

But he persisted, demanded a DNA test.

She ran.

He chased.

And that began the ten months of cat-and-mouse games.

If she hadn't bumped into that woman from the Ciragan Palace Hotel, Vittorio might never have found out about their son.

That had been her hope. That had been her plan.

The jet's bedroom door noiselessly opened and Vittorio stood in the doorway, his face shadowy in the dim lighting. "He's asleep?" Vitt asked quietly.

"Yes."

"Then come. Maria will be here any moment to spend the night with him—"

"I don't want to leave him!" she whispered.

"He'll be fine."

"Vitt, please. I've never slept away from him—"

"You'll have to sooner or later."

She glanced down at her baby in his blue pajamas. Her heart ached. "But not yet."

He studied her a moment, his expression inscrutable. "That's fine. We'll both sleep here then."

She'd thought at first he was joking—Vittorio was a man who loved his creature comforts—but it turned out he was serious, and left to go to his room to change into pajamas.

While Vittorio was gone, she slipped into the only nightgown she owned, a pink floral-sprigged flannel gown with a ruffled neckline, buttons down the front, and a long hem. It'd been a perfect gown for breast-feeding but it was far from glamorous or sexy.

Jillian brushed her teeth quickly and was just scooting into bed when Vittorio returned in dark gray pajama pants and a black silk robe. He glanced at her huddled in the bed and smiled briefly before turning out the light.

Nervously she turned on her side to face Joe's cot. With her eyes closed, she listened to Vitt approach, her ears straining to catch every sound he made from his heavy footsteps to the tug on the covers to the soft thud of his robe falling to the floor.

She felt the bed give on his side, felt the covers tug and then the warmth of his powerful body settle next to hers.

For a moment she couldn't breathe. She'd dreamed of this, of him, so many times since she'd run away from his villa in Bellagio, wanting so badly what she couldn't have.

Because she couldn't have him. It wasn't sane. He posed danger to her at every level.

But what was that expression? The heart wants what the heart wants?

And her heart had wanted him. Her heart had always wanted him.

"You can breathe," he said quietly, his voice pitched so only she could hear.

"I am."

"Barely."

She smiled in the dark even as her chest ached with fierce emotion. This was the Vittorio she'd wanted. This was the man who'd made her feel extraordinarily loved. "You don't need to worry about me," she whispered.

"Oh, but I think I do." His arm slid around her and he pulled her close against him. She felt his lips brush the back of her head. "Now relax. Sleep. Tomorrow will be here before you know it."

Miraculously, she did sleep. She must have drifted off right away because the next time she stirred, she was alone in the bed. Frowning, Jillian glanced at the clock on the narrow bedside table. Six hours had passed since she'd closed her eyes. Amazing because she never slept deeply, not anymore.

A soft knock sounded on the door and then the door opened. Maria entered with a tray. "Signor sent you coffee and juice and a breakfast pastry. He thought you might want something to eat before we land."

Jillian sat up, glanced at Joe who was stirring in his cot. "We're landing soon?"

Maria nodded and placed the tray next to Jillian on the bed. "In less than an hour."

Maria took Joe to the staff room to feed and dress him so that Jillian could have her coffee and dress in privacy.

Privacy felt like a luxury, Jillian thought as she nibbled on the breakfast roll between sips of coffee. But that was Vittorio's way—affluence, luxury, comfort. She'd forgotten just how posh his lifestyle was. She'd forgotten how decadent she'd felt in Bellagio in his lakeside villa with the stunning views of the mountains.

Dressed, she headed for the main cabin where Vittorio waited for her. "Did you sleep okay?" he asked her as she took a seat in one of the honey leather chairs opposite his.

"I did. Better than I have in months. Thank you."

"I didn't remember you being such a restless sleeper," he said, his long black eyelashes dropping to conceal his eyes. "You kicked and thrashed half of the night."

"Is that why you left so early this morning?"

"I stayed with you all night, only leaving so that I could have Maria bring you breakfast."

She flushed. "I didn't know."

"Yes. Apparently there's a great deal you don't know." He paused, studied her thoughtfully. "Just as there are many things I need to understand about you."

CHAPTER SIX

JILLIAN did not ask what he meant and Maria arrived with Joe just as the seat belt sign flashed on.

Jillian gratefully took Joe onto her lap and wrapped her arms around him. Blinding sunlight poured through the jet windows as the Boeing 737 dropped lower and lower until the jet's wheels finally touched ground. Once on the runway, she dropped a kiss on the top of her son's head, happy they'd landed safely.

As she kissed him, his cloud of soft black hair tickled her nose and she breathed in his sweet baby scent.

Feeling Vittorio's gaze, she glanced up, her eyes locking with his. He was sitting across the aisle from her and yet she could practically feel him. He had such a strong presence, a very physical energy that made her body hum even now.

"You have shadows under your eyes," he said.

"I shouldn't. I actually slept well last night."

"It sounds like you don't get a lot of sleep."

She shifted Joe in her arms. "Babies wake up a lot at night. And then of course, there's my need to check on him."

"You should have had more help with him."

Jillian knew what he was really saying—that if she'd come to him, she would have had help, she wouldn't have had to struggle on her own.

"It will be easier for you to sleep when Joseph is in his

own crib, in his own room," he added. "And he does have his own room at my house. There's space for Maria to sleep in the nursery should we need her to—"

"I like having Joe close at night," she interrupted. "I can't imagine not having him there."

"And I can't imagine making love to my wife if my son is present." His voice was firm, decisive. "Joseph will be fine in his own room. Trust me."

"So you've had a baby before?" she flashed, angered that he'd again start making decisions not just for Joe, but for her.

"No. But I can read a how-to-raise-a-baby book just as well as you, and I do have all those nieces and nephews."

She bit her lip to keep from replying sharply, and still struggling with her temper, turned her head to look out the window. It was a gorgeous clear morning. The sun was still rising and the sky stretched overhead, a lucid, cloudless blue. "You said I looked tired," she said. "Should I put some makeup on?"

"That's not necessary. You look fine. Just be yourself."

Ah, there was the dilemma. After falling into Vittorio's arms after so many months of running from him and fearing him, Jillian didn't even know who she was anymore. "As if it were that easy."

"It's not?"

Her lips twisted wryly. "No."

"Why not?"

She wanted to tell him she'd lived too many different lives in too many places. She wanted to share that more than once she'd sat frozen in a classroom or the cafeteria, terrified to open her mouth in the event she said the wrong thing. In the event she'd forgotten her part.

Lee. Carol. Anne. Jillian.

"Why isn't it?" Vitt asked, repeating his question.

She turned toward him, seeing his black tailored trousers,

the white shirt, the expensive black blazer. But then everything about him oozed money, success. "You've always lived in one place, and been raised around the same people. You've never had to be anyone but Vittorio d'Severano. It was different for me."

"You moved a lot when you were growing up?"

"Yes."

"Your father was in the military?"

She nearly laughed. Her father in the service? Her father an honorable man? *"No."*

"What did he do?"

Lied. Cheated. Backstabbed. But she couldn't say that. "Business. Sales. Things like that."

The jet had stopped taxiing to park at a small executive terminal.

"You never wanted to work with him?" Vitt asked, ignoring his flight crew as they prepared the aircraft for deplaning.

"No." She felt Joe wiggle on her lap, his small body warm and compact against hers and she glanced down at him, thinking there was so much she wanted for him, so much she wanted to give him if only she had the chance.

"What about you?" she asked Vitt as he unbuckled his seat belt and got to his feet. "Did your father expect you to go to work for him?"

Vitt towered above her, his expression somber. For a long moment he was silent before he gave his head a brief shake. "No. In fact, the opposite was true. He begged me to go somewhere else, do something different, but I wouldn't."

Her forehead furrowed. "Why not?"

Vitt shrugged as he reached for Joe and swung him into his arms. "I was a d'Severano. And my father needed me."

The door opened and sunlight filled the front cabin. Vittorio waited at the head of the stairs for Jillian before descending the staircase. Jillian descended more slowly, cautious in her high heels. She actually felt pulled together this morning in her brown sheath dress and chocolate suede pumps. All she needed was a great pair of sunglasses and she could pretend she was a movie star.

Vittorio's hand was on the small of her back as they started across the tarmac. A line of black town cars waited, each with tinted glass. Vittorio almost always traveled with escorts and bodyguards. He was rich. And he was a d'Severano. Therefore he could never be too careful.

They were nearly to the cars when a door opened on one of the black sedans. A slim blonde woman emerged.

Vittorio stopped in his tracks, his expression hardening. "She never listens," he said, shaking his head. "I told her not to come."

Jillian shot a swift glance at the sophisticated blonde in the pale blue suit. "Who is she?"

He sighed. "My mother."

Jillian stiffened. "Your mother?"

"She's what I like to call an independent thinker."

Until this moment, Jillian had been almost excited about arriving in Catania. She enjoyed travel and usually loved the moment she stepped off an airplane, thrilled by the sense of freedom and possibilities that came from being somewhere new. Every place had a different feel and unique energy. But all sense of wonder abruptly disappeared.

Vittorio's hand remained on her back. "This might be rough," he said. "But just remind yourself that you will survive."

Her heart fell. His mother sounded awful. "You're telling me her bark is worse than her bite?"

"No." His full sensual mouth twisted, dark eyes narrowed. "I'm telling you that no one yet has died from her bite."

"And that is really not very comforting."

He smiled suddenly, dark eyes glinting with humor before

he dropped a kiss on her lips. "Oh, she also thinks we're radiantly happy, and completely in love. Can you manage that?"

She pressed her lips together, mouth tingling from his brief kiss. She wished he'd kiss her again. There was something dangerously addictive about his mouth. "I'll try."

He smiled again. "Good luck." And then they were walking once more, closing the distance between them and the waiting cars.

Jillian's high heels made faint clicking sounds on the tarmac but her gaze was fixed on Vittorio's mother. She looked youthful, even glamorous in her ice-blue suit trimmed in a blue, aqua and cream braid, and matching high heels the same color. She wore her hair in a loose chignon, a style which highlighted her elegant features.

Jillian stood back as Vitt embraced her warmly and then introduced her to his son. How could this woman be Vitt's mother?

But Vitt was turning to Jillian now, and extending a hand. "*Madre*, this is my wife, Jill," he said, drawing Jillian all the way forward. "Jill, my mother, Theresa d'Severano."

Up close Jillian could see that Theresa d'Severano wasn't quite as young as Jillian had first thought, but neither did she look like a woman in her mid-fifties. Jillian didn't know if it was genetics or technology, but Theresa could have easily passed for Vitt's sister.

Suddenly Jillian didn't feel as pulled together as she had just a few minutes ago and wished she'd taken the time to put on a little makeup before stepping off the plane. But it was too late for lipstick. All she could do was make the best impression possible. Summoning her confidence as well as a warm smile, Jillian extended her hand. "It's a pleasure to meet you, Mrs. d'Severano."

Theresa gave her a long, level look, the expression in her

blue eyes cool. She ignored Jillian's hand. "You're the woman that trapped Vittorio."

So that's what they think happened. Vittorio, the adored oldest son and the apple of his mother's eye, had been ensnared by a villainous American gold digger. Jillian only wished she was half as sneaky and manipulative as his family imagined.

She dropped her hand and struggled to keep her smile. "I've heard a lot about you."

His mother's smile turned positively glacial. "Odd. I never heard a word about you."

Vittorio gestured toward the car. "Mother, why don't we continue our conversation on the drive home?" he suggested pleasantly even though his mouth was set hard.

His mother patted his arm. "Why don't you and the baby take one car, and Jill and I will take another? This way she and I can spend a little bit of time getting to know each other."

Jillian swallowed, thinking it was one of the worst ideas she'd ever heard but she couldn't very well say that.

"Jill?" Vitt said, looking at her. "What do you prefer?"

It was good of him to give her a choice. It sounded like the right thing to say, but clearly he didn't understand that Jillian couldn't refuse his mother's suggestion without appearing ungracious. She forced a smile. "I'd love to ride with your mother," she said. "Sounds like fun."

"It's probably a good idea," he agreed smoothly. "This way you'll have an ally on your side before you meet the rest of the family."

Jillian then had no choice but to follow his mother into her black sedan, even as her gaze strayed to her baby in Vitt's arms. She should be with Vitt and Joe. She should be traveling with them, not Vitt's mom.

"Have you ever been to Sicily?" Theresa asked as they each took position on opposite ends of the leather seat.

The chauffeur started the car and pulled away from the other sedans. Jillian forced herself to focus on Vitt's mother. The interior of the car was dark and cool and she needed a moment for her eyes to adjust after the bright morning sunlight. "No. I'm sorry I haven't."

Theresa tapped her nails on the door's metal handle. "Is your family Sicilian?"

"No."

"Italian?"

Her father was, yes, but she couldn't tell Theresa that. "German and Scottish, with a dab of Irish and a hint of French."

His mother regarded her steadily, her focus sharp. "You've been to Bellagio."

"Yes."

"The villa is beautiful."

"Extraordinary."

"Did you drive his Lamborghini?"

"No, the Ferrari."

"It's a nice life, isn't it? The cars, the houses, expensive jewelry."

They were back to the perception that Jillian was a gold digger. Jillian didn't know whether she should laugh or cry. She cared about many things, but money wasn't one of them. "You do your Vittorio a disservice. He's brilliant, devastatingly attractive and without a doubt, the most complex man I've ever met."

"But the money *is* nice."

Jillian kept her expression pleasant. "If I wanted a rich husband, I could have had a rich husband without the complications of a difficult family."

Theresa stiffened, her eyes narrowing as she fell silent.

Jillian realized she'd probably made a gross tactical error, but there was no going back now. All she could do was try to hold her own, push on and see this brutal conversation to the end. "But my family is no better," she said awkwardly, trying to make amends. "They don't approve of Vitt any more than you approve of me."

"You make it sound like you and Vittorio are two starcrossed lovers."

She shrugged lightly. "I suppose there are shades of Romeo and Juliet in our story, but hopefully without the tragic ending."

"Why don't your parents approve of Vittorio?"

Ah, Theresa didn't like that, did she? "They're aware that he and I come from different backgrounds, and perhaps have different values."

Theresa sat very still, her hands motionless in her lap. "Different values?"

"As you just pointed out, I'm neither Sicilian or Italian, and although I was raised Catholic, I rarely go to Mass now and yet from what I understand, your family is quite devout."

"So why did he marry you?"

"Love."

Theresa stared at her for the longest moment before smiling mockingly. "And you actually expect me to believe any of that drivel?"

Jillian opened her mouth to protest, but Theresa leaned toward Jillian and calmly, ruthlessly continued, "You don't think I have my own connections? You don't think I ask questions? I know you only just got married. And I know you didn't want to marry my son—you only married him to keep your son."

Jillian bit down into her lip, stunned.

But Theresa wasn't done yet. Her cool blue gaze swept Jillian's ashen face. "You can play whatever game you want to play with Vittorio, Jill, but don't play games with me." She paused, before bluntly saying, "Your entire relationship is a sham, isn't it?"

"No."

"It seems like one to me—"

"But it's not your relationship. It's mine. I adore Vittorio. I always have."

"So why am I only meeting you now, a year after my grandson's birth?"

Jillian sat tall, her chin tilted up. "I don't see how that is any of your business."

"I'm his mother!"

"And I'm his wife."

The rest of the trip passed in tense silence. Twenty-five minutes after leaving Catania, they reached Vittorio's hometown of Paterno. Catania, Sicily's second largest city, was crowded and noisy, a sprawling urban city with a questionable reputation, whereas small, serene Paterno lay surrounded by citrus orchards with the protective tower and walls of the d'Severano family's Norman castle standing guard.

It was a bright, clear morning with a stunning blue sky and the drive from the outskirts of Paterno to the castle entrance provided breathtaking views of both Mt Etna and the Simeto Valley.

Jillian and Theresa arrived first at the castle and were just stepping from their car, smoothing skirts and adjusting hemlines without once looking at each other, when the second black sedan arrived. Emerging from the back of his sedan, Vitt lifted Joseph out and then joined his mother and Jillian before the stone steps that led to the castle's massive front doors.

"How was the drive?" he asked, glancing from his mother's stony expression to the tight press of Jillian's lips.

"Good," Jillian said, her voice cracking.

"Not my choice of words, but we're both here, aren't we?" his mother retorted, one of her elegant winged eyebrows arching higher before turning around and walking away, her thin back ramrod-straight.

Vittorio watched his mother climb the pale stone stairs before turning back to Jill. "Sounds like an interesting trip," he said drily, eyes glinting again.

Of course he'd find his mother amusing. "It was," she agreed, taking Joe from Vitt and giving him a kiss.

"Did she ask a lot of questions?"

"Yes."

"Was she direct?"

"As well as rude." She took a deep breath, shook her head. "She doesn't like me at all."

"She doesn't know you."

"Well, she certainly doesn't think we should be together."

"You felt the same way yesterday," he retorted with a smile. "Now enough about my mother. Let me show you and Joseph around your new home."

From the immense twelfth-century walls, Jillian had imagined the interior would be dark and severe. Instead the castle had the feel of an airy Mediterranean villa. Everything was light and bright, walls and upholstery and floors all finished in cool, calming shades of white, sea-foam green and ethereal blue.

Because Joe was growing tired, Vittorio kept the tour brief, but Jillian didn't need a lot of description to be dazzled by Vitt's home. There was a sensual beauty to his castle, a warmth that permeated the old stones, thick walls and high-ceilinged rooms.

As they climbed stairs into towers, crossed terraces to view private gardens, Jillian caught whiffs of the heady perfume from the flowering citrus groves below the castle and felt the warmth of the gentle April sunshine as it cascaded over the weathered rock walls and surfaces.

Returning to the impressive staircase, they arrived on the third floor consisting of Vitt's suite of rooms and the newly renovated nursery for their son.

Jillian paused inside the nursery door, eyes widening at the charming ocean theme. The airy, spacious nursery had a wall of windows flooding the carpeted floor with sunshine and bright light reflected off the walls painted with fanciful fish. "You did all this for Joe?"

"Why wouldn't I?"

"I mean, it's just so perfect…."

"Did you think I wouldn't provide for my son?"

"No! Of course not." She shifted Joe in her arms. "I've never once questioned your desire or ability to provide for Joe. I know you could give him anything."

"As long as it's material."

She fell silent, realizing she'd said the wrong thing.

"Because that's all I'm good for," he added in the same velvet soft tone. "Money. Connections. Prestige."

She blushed. "You're putting words in my mouth," she protested huskily, setting a wiggling Joe on his feet. The baby had spotted the sapphire dolphin rocking horse in the corner and was toddling fast toward the dolphin to climb on its back.

"But isn't the money and prestige part true? You wanted me, enjoyed me, until you discovered I wasn't your perfect prince and then you ran from me, disappearing without a word."

"I'm sorry. Forgive me."

"Apology not accepted."

"Please, Vitt."

"Please, what? This nursery has sat here empty for ten months. For ten months I searched for you, spending hundreds of thousands of dollars hiring investigators and detectives and following up on every lead possible. For ten months I waited to meet my son." He leaned against one of the bookcases flanking the tall paned glass windows, his strong profile silhouetted by the bright sunlight. "And every day I thought, the only reason my son isn't here, is because you, Jill Smith, wouldn't let him."

She felt her face grow hot. Put like that, she was a horrible person. But he didn't know the whole story, and as much as she wanted to tell him, she didn't think she could. At least not yet. At least, not until she knew for a fact that she could trust him. "I am sorry, Vittorio."

He made a rough disgusted sound. "Let's be honest. You're not sorry you kept Joseph from me. You're sorry I found you. Only you're too much a coward to admit it."

Jillian's face burned with shame, because Vittorio was right. She was a coward. A pathetic coward. But if it meant she could protect Joe, and remain with Joe, then she'd do whatever she had to. "Maybe," she admitted softly.

"Why did you do it, Jill? Why keep my son from me? You had to know I'd be good to him. You had to know I'd love him. I always treated you well. You trusted me, too, and when you slept, you always slept close to me, pressed to my side."

She hated how her eyes suddenly felt gritty and dry. She hated that she could still remember how she'd felt with him, too. Loved. Safe. So very secure. "That was before," she answered faintly.

"Before?" he repeated, as if amused. Faint creases appeared at the corner of his eyes.

"Yes."

"Before what?"

He was still smiling but she realized she'd misread him. He wasn't amused. He was far from amused.

Jillian held her breath, the air bottled in her lungs, aware that she was walking on thin ice and she had no idea how to extract herself.

But Vittorio wasn't waiting for the ice to crack. He was going to shatter it himself. The corner of his mouth lifted. "Before you invented a world where I played the villain?"

She stared across the room at him. "I invented nothing. I dreamed up nothing. It's all there, Vittorio. It's all there on the internet."

"It's not true."

"There are dozens of stories and articles, Vitt."

"And you believe everything you read on the internet?"

"Not always."

"But you believed this…whatever it was you read about me?"

"Why would people lie?"

He studied her with his dark, fathomless eyes, the sensual curve of his mouth making her feel hurt and longing and desire and pain.

She'd loved his mouth, loved the shape of that mouth and everything it made her feel—physically, emotionally. He'd always made her feel so much and until she'd discovered the truth about him, it'd been so good. She'd felt so good. After so many years she'd felt whole. And then the truth emerged and she shattered all over again.

"Why indeed?" he mocked.

She waited for him to say something else. Waited for him to explain or defend or help her make sense of this life of his. He didn't.

She balled her hands into fists. "So now's your chance. Tell me. Tell me the truth. Are you…?"

"Am I what?"

"You know."

His head tipped to the side. "Do you realize you're in danger of sounding obsessive?"

His mockery infuriated her. "This is serious," she snapped.

"You've watched too many Hollywood movies."

"I know what I know."

"And just what do you know, *Jill*? You seem to be an expert on masquerades and games and charades."

She shivered at his tone. What if he knew more than she thought he did? What if he knew what she hadn't wanted him to know?

What then?

And what would he do with the information?

But she wouldn't let herself go there, not now, not yet. Instead she locked her knees for courage. "I know Sicily has a long, complicated history with the mafia. I know that the Italian government has tried for years to rid Sicily of the mafia but without great success."

"And why do you think?" he asked, watching her from beneath his thickly fringed lashes.

"Because by all reports, the mafia leaders are very clever."

He held her gaze, his dark eyes searching hers. "Or perhaps the mafia does not exist."

So that's how he wanted to do this. They were to pretend she was misinformed, confused, off base.

He wanted her to believe the mafia didn't exist. He was asking her to accept that organized crime was a Hollywood fabrication. He was asking the impossible.

She wasn't that girl. She knew better. She knew the truth.

Jillian had lived through things, experienced things most people only read about in books or watched on TV. Her father, while presenting a charming face to the world, had the callous heart of a killer. Her *father*.

"Is that what you want me to believe?" she choked.

"You must have had one miserable childhood, because you're completely incapable of trusting another."

"I'm completely incapable of trusting you."

"Just me?"

"Just you," she retorted, even though it was a lie. She didn't trust many people. She certainly didn't trust powerful men and still didn't know why she'd decided to trust Vitt nearly two years ago.

"Why?"

"You know why."

"The *Mafioso* thing again?" he asked, sounding bored.

"Yes, that. It's never gone away. It will never go away—"

"Which is a dilemma, isn't it? Because now you're my wife. Married to the mob. What will you do?"

"I don't know," she answered, throwing her head back, temper blazing even as tears shimmered in her eyes. "None of this was supposed to happen. It's the worst thing that could have happened."

"Why?"

"Because it'd kill me, Vitt, it would if my son grew up and became someone like you."

CHAPTER SEVEN

It'd kill me if my son grew up and became someone like you.

It'd been two hours since Jillian had said the words but they still echoed in Vitt's head.

It would kill her if her son were like him...it would kill her...

Unbelievably hurtful words, especially considering they came from the mother of his child.

The worst of it was that she didn't know him. She couldn't seem to see who he really was. But he wasn't used to explaining himself, or opening his family or life to scrutiny.

Frankly, he didn't care what people thought of him. And he answered to no one.

Because no one could touch him, although in the beginning everyone had tried. Prime ministers, presidents, parliaments, governments. Police in every country.

But what could they do to him? To the d'Severano family? What crime had he committed? What crime could they pin on his father? None.

Yet Vittorio was still feared, hated, loved and loathed. He didn't even try to justify his behavior, or contradict the rumors or lies anymore. It was a waste of time, a waste of energy. Life was short. He would love it.

And yet Jill's words had struck a nerve. A very sensitive

nerve. Because he was not a bad man, or an evil man, or a violent man. He, like his father, had spent his life righting past wrongs, as well as building new relationships with people, businesses, world leaders.

He did have family members who were connected to the mafia, but he wasn't one of them. Nor was his father. Nor would his son be.

Because you didn't have to be crooked to be powerful. And you didn't have to resort to pressure or violence to be influential. His success stemmed directly from his work ethic, his focus and his value system.

So let Jill Smith, the twenty-six year old American he'd just made his wife, say what she wanted. He knew the truth. He knew who he was. He knew what he was.

But in his heart, her words did hurt.

Jillian held Joe's hand as they walked in the rose garden after his afternoon nap. He toddled happily from bush to bush, savoring the sunshine and colorful petals and sweet scent of the antique roses.

Jillian talked to him and crouched down to help him smell different blossoms but her insides churned, her heart felt heavy.

She'd said something awful to Vitt earlier and she couldn't forget what she'd said, or Vitt's expression as she'd said it.

It'd kill me if he were to grow up and become like you....
Such cruel, hurtful words.

But she hadn't meant to hurt him. She was just being honest. Just sharing her fear.

Her father's crimes still horrified her, and she believed more than ever that the world needed good people. The world needed men who were strong. Courageous.

Compassionate.

That's the kind of man she wanted Joe to be one day. That's

the kind of man she'd thought Vitt was. Until she'd looked the d'Severanos up on Google and found out the truth.

Crouching next to a pink rosebush, Jillian held a soft open flower up for Joe to smell it. He pressed his face into the petals. "Mmm," he said.

"Smells good, doesn't it?" she said.

He smiled up at her, his eyes deeply blue, his expression trusting.

Her heart ached all over again. She owed Vittorio an apology. She needed to let him know she'd been wrong to say something so unkind, especially in front of their son. Hopefully she could talk to him before they met his family for dinner. She wouldn't feel better until she apologized.

Footsteps sounded on the walk and Jillian looked up to see Maria approach.

"Is it time for dinner already?" Jillian asked.

Maria shook her head. "Signor sent me to tell you that he is not eating at home tonight. He said that he'll have dinner sent to you and Joe in your suite, and that you'll meet his family tomorrow."

Jillian straightened. "Did he say when he'd be back?"

The nanny shook her head. "No. But he may not return tonight. It's possible he'll remain in Catania until tomorrow."

Jillian's heart fell. "What?"

"He has a big apartment there, not far from his office. I've never seen it but I've heard that it's at the top of a building and very nice. In English I think you call it a penthouse." Maria bobbed her head and then excused herself, returning to the house.

For a moment Jillian just watched Maria walk and then driven by some dark, murky emotion, Jillian scooped up Joe and chased after Maria. "Is Signor still here?" she asked, catching up with Maria just inside the door.

The castle felt cool and shadowy after the afternoon sun.

"I think so," Maria answered. "He might even still be upstairs."

Jillian left Joe with Maria and dashed up the stairs, her high heels tapping against the polished stone floor. She reached their bedroom just as Vittorio was turning off the light.

"Where are you going?" she asked breathlessly.

"To Catania. I have some business to take care of."

"You're going to your office?"

"Does it matter?"

She searched his dark eyes yet his expression was so completely shuttered she couldn't see what he was thinking. "Yes."

"I will be going to my office, yes, among other places."

"Do you conduct most of your meetings at the office?"

"Not necessarily." He gazed down at her, lips curling in a sardonic smile. "Worried that I'll be conducting illicit business in dark alleys, Jill?"

"No."

There was a moment of tense silence before Vittorio shook his head. "And you call me a liar." His smile grew, his dark eyes glittering with anger. "But I don't have time for this, as interesting as it is. Have a good night. Don't wait up for me. I'm not sure when I'll return."

"You're not coming back tonight?"

"I don't know. Haven't decided."

"Vitt," she protested, reaching out to touch his coat sleeve.

He glanced down at her hand resting on his dark coat and then into her face. "Don't even try to pretend that you'll miss me, Jill."

She flushed, her cheeks burning with heat. "It's only our first night here. I don't know anyone. I barely know my way around."

"You have our son. You know Maria. That should be

enough." He paused, considered her. "It has to be enough. Because that's all you really have."

She felt as if he'd slapped her. Her eyes watered. Her blush deepened, her skin burning from her chest to her brow. "You don't need to be cruel."

"I see. You can say whatever you want, but I have to play nice?"

"I'm sorry about earlier—"

"No you're not. You're never sorry. You're spoiled and selfish and incredibly self-centered. And since you're so big on the truth, let me tell you the truth. You are the absolute last woman in the world I would have picked to be my wife."

"You didn't used to think that—"

"Because I didn't know you. But I do now."

She buried her hands behind her back as tears filled her eyes, and then pressed her lips together to keep them from trembling.

"Truth hurts," he said bitterly, "doesn't it?"

"I never meant to hurt you," she said, "but you're enjoying being cruel."

"I don't enjoy being cruel. But I will give it to you straight. This isn't the kind of marriage I envisioned, just as you aren't the kind of wife I wanted. But it doesn't matter now. I deal in reality, not in fantasy or fairy tales. We slept together. You became pregnant. I accept my responsibility."

How could he be so cold when her heart felt as though it were on fire? "How good of you," she murmured. "How very mature."

He shrugged. "There's no love here between us. There never will be, at least, not now. So we will focus on our son. We'll sleep together on occasion. Have sex when the mood strikes. Put on a good face in front of my family. But that's it. Understand? That's all you'll get from me, and that's all I want from you."

She blinked, looked away, battled to keep control because it felt like he was taking a knife to her, again and again. "Stop it."

"Stop what?"

"Torturing me."

"Torturing you is the last thing on my mind. I'm merely clarifying our relationship, defining the parameters before we have to function in front of my family and the rest of the world."

"And those parameters?"

"You belong to me in the bedroom. The rest of your life is your own."

"I am not an object."

"Agreed. You are my wife. You will fulfill your conjugal duties. But you are free to shop, and travel, and make female friends of your choosing."

"Female?" she flashed, glancing up at him, tears still matting her lashes.

"Only female. I will tear apart any man that comes within ten feet of you. You are my wife. You are a d'Severano. You'd best remember that."

"You must enjoy having so much power when I have none."

"You don't need power. You have me."

"To think for me, speak for me and force me to lie in your bed!"

"I shall never need force to get you into my bed. I proved that point yesterday. But if you'd care for a refresher—"

"Not necessary, but thank you."

He smiled mockingly and reached for his tie, loosening it slightly. "Maybe I do have time for a quickie."

"No."

"No?"

The pale green bedroom walls felt as though they were

about to close in. "I mean, not like this. Not a quickie. It won't be right."

"And what would be right? Romance? Candles? Soft music in the background?"

"You're so angry."

"I am."

She trembled inwardly, not out of fear, but shock and pain. She didn't want him angry with her, not like this, not when they'd once been so happy together. Maybe they only had two weeks, but those two weeks had been the happiest of her life and she wondered if they could maybe be happy again. If they could just sort out their past. If they could just figure out the future. How they'd do that, she didn't know, but she had to have hope. Had to believe they could make a real marriage out of this, otherwise, how did one live in a loveless marriage? How did one live with so much? How would she survive the next seventeen years?

"I don't want you angry, Vittorio. And I do want to fix this…make amends. I don't know how yet, but will you at least let me try?"

For an endless stretch of time he said nothing. Then he reached out to her, his palm sliding down her neck, his fingers curving to fit her nape with his thumb at her earlobe. "And how would you do that?" he murmured huskily, stroking the hollow beneath her earlobe.

Her pulse leaped at his touch. She licked her lips as her mouth dried. "I would try to remind you that we can be good together. That we could be happy."

"Where?"

"Anywhere."

His dark eyes held hers, the brown irises hot, glowing with tiny shards of amber and gold. "Does that include the bedroom?"

"Yes."

"You're offering me your body."

"Yes," she answered, her voice low.

His dark eyes flared with heat and immediate carnal desire. "And what will you do for me when I am in your bed?"

He was binding her heart with a chain. "Whatever it is you want your wife to do."

Vitt's hand slid down her neck to her collarbone and then over the middle of her chest, into the V between her breasts. "Anything I want?"

His hand was warm, so warm on her chest. Her breasts swelled, heavy, her nipples hardening. "You said I was to be obedient."

"What a good wife you intend to be," he taunted, clasping her jaw in both his hands, lifting her face to his. He held her face up, examining every inch as if she were a beautiful thing he'd bought at market and he was now eager to inspect his purchase. After an endless, scorching scrutiny, he dipped his head, covered her lips with his, and kissed her deeply. His tongue probed her mouth, tasting, savoring the softness and heat within.

Jillian shuddered, heat exploding in her middle, coursing through her veins.

His tongue stroked the inside of her lower lip, flaming nerve endings everywhere. His teeth, straight, white, nipped at her lip and heat flared from her womb to her limbs.

She was melting, dissolving in his hands.

And then he drew her tongue into his mouth and sucked the tip, the sucking sensation tight and rhythmic, reminding her of his body thrusting into hers, making her back arch, her hips tilt, her body shaping to his.

His hands slid up into her hair, his fingers dragging across her scalp. He was waking her, warming her, fanning the empty aching need.

And still he kissed her, his knee parting her thighs, pressing up against her sensitive flesh and she grew hot, wet, needy in response.

Jillian slid her hands up his chest, feeling his heart beat beneath her hands as she kissed him back, her skin hot and sensitive, her body taut with desire.

Long moments passed and then he lifted his head. He gazed down into her eyes a long moment and stroked her flushed, warm cheek. "I think I will claim what is mine."

He unzipped her dress and peeled it off over her head before unhooking her bra and casting it on top of the discarded dress. Her panties followed along with her slim chocolate heels.

Once he had her naked, he dropped her not all that gently onto the enormous bed. With his dark gaze fixed on her, he shed his own clothes and then joined her on the bed, pushing her back to straddle her hips.

This time there was no foreplay. This was a lesson in ownership, a display of possession. He possessed her, too, stretching her out beneath him, his hands holding her wrists down above her head, his chest crushing her full breasts, his strong thighs holding her slim thighs apart as he entered her, and then filled her, driving deep into her body, again and again.

She was warm and slick, his shaft thick and hard, and he stroked her relentlessly, creating a maddening friction that was so pleasurable it almost caused pain.

With each of his thrusts she tightened her inner muscles around him, wanting to hold him, wanting to keep him with her in an attempt to meet that wonderful and yet terrible need he created.

As he filled her, her head spun, and her senses swam with the dizzying pleasure of it all. Making love to him had always made her emotions feel wildly out of control. Today was no different. She craved him. She hated him. She needed him. She wanted him. She wanted him like she'd never wanted anyone or anything. And when together like this, skin against skin, warmth to warmth, heartbeat to heartbeat, she didn't think she could possibly ever want anything more.

This was intimacy, and closeness, connection as she'd never known it. Together like this, she felt whole. Comforted. Cherished. The lovemaking was such perfection it made her eyes sting and her heart ache. She never wanted it to end. Not even tonight.

Long before she was ready, her body betrayed her, nerves and muscles coiling into an explosive physical climax that triggered his. She sighed as he released into her, her body still sensitive and shuddering with pleasure. How could sex be so right with him when everything else was so wrong?

For a moment she allowed herself to relax into him, savoring the feel of his hard, lean body. And then he withdrew.

As always, she felt bereft.

As always her heart ached, wanting, needing more.

He turned onto his side, pulled her up against him, his arm over her chest holding her close to him. She let him, too, because when they were together like this, she did need him. She needed him more than she'd ever needed anyone. Her life had been lonely. Her father's problems had eclipsed everyone else's needs. When Vittorio loved—even if only with his body—she felt good. And safe. Safer than she felt with anyone else.

But sex, even slow and leisurely, didn't last forever. It always ended. And the afterglow always ended. And then she was swamped with all the overwhelming emotions again.

Emptiness. Pain. Hopelessness. Sadness.

And so when he wrapped his arm around her, his forearm warm and snug against her breast, she unsteadily exhaled and inhaled and exhaled again to keep the tears from falling.

How could she mistrust him and yet need him so much?

How could he make her feel so vulnerable? No one else made her feel this way. Why did he?

* * *

Lying in the bedroom's semidarkness, with the last lingering rays of sunlight fading from the sky, Vittorio felt Jill's chest rise and fall, a silent hiccup of emotion that she never acknowledged, and always refused to discuss. Suppressing a sigh, he drew her small frame closer to him, her soft round breasts pressed to his arm.

She was so full of secrets and her secrets wore on her. He'd known many men who lived in the shadows, clandestine lives filled with cloak-and-dagger games, but those men reveled in their furtive behavior, thriving on danger, thriving on power. Jill didn't.

He'd once wished she'd tell him what troubled her. He no longer cared. Or that's what he told himself.

But when her narrow rib cage rose and fell with a deep shuddering breath, his own chest grew tight.

In Bellagio everything had been easy between them. Not just the sex, but the connection, the conversation, the friendship they'd been building. He'd trusted her. He'd believed she was honest, true and real.

Turned out nothing about her was honest or real. Not her name. Not her past. Not even her hair color.

His meeting tonight was with one of his detectives. The detective had learned what he'd called "significant details" of Jill's past.

Tonight in Catania he'd discover who she really was.

Tonight could change everything.

And so he held her closer, held her as if he could possibly keep bad news from changing the fragile tie between them.

Maybe in his own way, he still loved her a little.

"When I first saw you on the cliff, I thought perhaps you were wearing a wig," he said quietly, his voice rough with passion and emotion he'd never share. "But it's not a wig. You dyed it."

She lay still in his arms. "Yes."

"How have you perfected so many different disguises?"

"Theater. I performed in all the high school plays and musicals. I loved it so much that I went to Gonzaga as a theater arts major."

"I thought you studied hotel management."

"I did. I graduated with a degree in hotel management, but initially I wanted to be an actress."

"Why?"

She took a deep slow breath. Her voice wasn't entirely steady. "I wanted to be someone else."

Vittorio stayed with her another half hour and then wordlessly he pulled away and left the bed. She lay on her side facing the wall listening to Vittorio dress.

He was leaving.

Leaving her.

She told herself she didn't care. She squeezed her eyes closed, trying to ignore the slide of fabric and the scrape of zipper. Then came a moment of quiet. She felt Vitt's hesitation. Felt him standing over the bed, gazing down at her. She didn't turn to him, or speak. She kept her eyes closed pretending to sleep.

Then he walked away and the bedroom door opened. She opened her eyes then, looked toward the door and the hallway. A ray of light fell across the bedroom floor and she glimpsed Vittorio's hard, handsome profile and his shoulder before the door closed, shrouding the bedroom in darkness once again.

For long minutes she lay on her back, thinking but not thinking. Feeling but not feeling. Doing her best to close her own door on her inner turmoil.

She couldn't let herself feel. Couldn't analyze a single emotion. Couldn't go inward because if she did, she'd fall apart.

Every time she was with Vitt it felt so right, so why did it have to be so wrong?

* * *

In Catania Vittorio met with the American private investigator at his office. It was nine o'clock and the office was closed, all lights off except for the executive suite that housed Vittorio's office.

The detective, a former FBI agent, sat across the desk from Vitt, a notepad open on his lap, telling Vitt everything he'd discovered.

He'd discovered a great deal.

It required all of Vitt's self-control to remain seated with his expression neutral while the detective revealed everything he'd discovered about Vittorio's new wife.

April Holliday wasn't Jillian's only alias. Jillian Smith was an alias, as well. There were three other aliases before she had become Jillian Smith at age sixteen.

She'd been in the U.S. government's witness protection program for fourteen years, had moved numerous times and changed her looks and name repeatedly because her family's safety had been repeatedly compromised.

"She had four different identities on file with the government," the detective said, glancing briefly at his notes. "She was creating that fifth one—April Holliday—when we located her in Carmel. But April Holliday wasn't a government-issued identity. It was one she'd created on her own to hide from you."

Vitt's brow lowered. "Is she still part of the witness protection program?"

"She is supposed to be. The rest of her family still is."

"Where is her family?"

"Parents are in Florida. The exact location isn't known."

"Who are they?"

The detective shook his head. "That is the one piece of information missing from her file." He leaned forward, slid a sheet of paper across the desk toward Vittorio. On the paper he'd listed all of Jill's aliases, including her schools and studies and the different addresses from the time she was twelve until now. "There is nothing I could find that gives her birth name, or her parents' original names. Like Jillian, her family goes by Smith, and has used Smith for a number of years. We do know that the entire family, a family of four—mother, father and two daughters—was placed in the program fourteen years ago but we don't know why."

Vittorio calmly studied the paper in his hand, his relaxed features revealing none of his inner tension. There was a reason Jill had run from him in Bellagio. She'd heard the word *Mafioso* whispered and disappeared like a thief in the night. And she'd kept running until he'd found her. But she remained terrified of him. She'd made it clear she didn't trust him, or believe that he wasn't connected to the mafia. She'd said so several times.

She had to be linked to the mob herself. Had to have insider knowledge. Why else would she be so completely unable to trust him?

"There is nothing here of her original identity," he said, glancing at the former FBI agent. "According to this paper, she didn't even exist before she was twelve."

"That's right. Everything in her file that would link her to a birth name, birthplace, or birth date was completely erased."

Vitt kept his expression neutral. "Is this normal protocol for the United States' protection program?"

"No."

"But you've seen this before?"

The detective hesitated. "Yes. There are two incidences when I've seen this happen—when the government is protecting a foreign spy, or a high-ranking member of an organized crime family."

There it was. The connection to organized crime. Vitt had

known it in his gut, but wondered why it'd taken him so long to see it.

"So what do you think we're dealing with?" Vitt asked, sounding bored.

"She's the daughter of an American mob boss."

Vitt felt hard and cold all the way through. It's what he'd been thinking, but somehow it sounded a thousand times worse spoken aloud. "Are there many in the American government's witness protection program?"

"A half dozen."

"Anyone you view a particular threat?"

"One or two, although Frankie Giordano is the one the government is most protective of. He sold out the entire Detroit operation, and Detroit was linked to nearly every other operation."

Vitt nodded slowly. "Which means Giordano gave up everyone."

"Yes."

"If his whereabouts were discovered, he'd be a dead man."

The detective closed his notebook. "As would his family."

CHAPTER EIGHT

JILLIAN woke up with sunlight pouring through the windows. She hadn't drawn the drapes last night when she'd gone to bed. Instead she'd stayed up late, leafing through Italian *Vogue* and French *Elle*, magazines Maria had loaned her, waiting for Vittorio to return.

He hadn't, though.

He'd remained out all night. Or if he had returned, he'd slept elsewhere.

The fact that he'd stayed away worried her. He'd been so upset with her yesterday. And she knew she deserved his anger, but she was also desperate to patch things up. She didn't know how to live in his house and be shunned by him.

Jillian bathed and dressed quickly before heading to Joe's nursery to check on him. He wasn't there so she went in search of him, knowing he had to be with Maria.

But he wasn't with Maria. He was with his father having breakfast on the terrace just off the dining room.

The soft pink-tinged morning light painted the terrace's pale stones rose and gold. Large clay pots lined the terrace, and beyond the balustrade the valley and snow-capped Mt Etna dominated the view.

"Good morning," Jillian said huskily, turning her back on green-and-yellow hills dotted with orchards and farmhouses to face Vitt and Joe.

"'Morning," Vitt answered, breaking up a breakfast roll into little pieces for Joe who sat in a tall antique high chair at Vitt's elbow.

She noticed that he barely looked at her and his tone bordered on cold. "May I join you?" she asked uncertainly even as she leaned over to give Joe a kiss.

"It's your home," he said, sounding completely disinterested.

She breathed in Joe's warmth and baby scent for courage before straightening and taking a seat at the glass-topped table.

Kitchen staff immediately appeared to place another setting for her and offer her a choice of espresso or American style drip coffee. Jillian chose the drip coffee and then clutched her hands in her lap to hide her nervousness.

"When did you get back?" she asked, struggling to keep her voice light and normal.

"Last night."

Her heart fell and ridiculous tears burned the back of her eyes. So where had he slept? And why hadn't he come to their room? "How did your meeting go?"

"It was interesting."

"That's good." She forced her lips up into a brittle smile and then caught Joe's eye. He was staring at her as he fed himself a bite of the bread. She smiled more warmly even as her eyes felt grittier, saltier. Please God, don't let her cry.

"Tell me about your family," Vitt said abruptly, leaning back in his chair. "You never talk about them."

"I…I'm not sure what you want to know."

"Tell me about your father. You said he was a businessman. Sales, I think you said."

She nodded woodenly. "Yes."

"And you moved a lot growing up?"

"Yes."

His eyes narrowed a fraction. "Where were you born?"

"De—" Jillian broke off, bit her tongue, realizing she'd come dangerously close to telling him the very things the government had insisted she never share. "Dallas."

"Dallas?" he repeated, head tipping to the side. "Which hospital?"

"I don't remember. I'd have to ask my mother."

"And where is she?"

"In a retirement community in Florida."

"We should invite them out for our wedding."

"They don't…they don't…like to fly."

"Don't you want your father to give you away?"

She squirmed. "Of course I would, but they don't travel much and they wouldn't be comfortable here."

His lips curved. "Here in our home?"

"No."

"You mean, here in Sicily?"

"No. That's not what I mean."

"So what do you mean, Jill?"

Completely flustered, she bit down into her lower lip, chewed the tender skin. "I'm not close with my parents," she said at last. "I haven't seen them in years."

"They've never met Joseph then?"

She shook her head. "They don't even know he exists."

"I'm shocked."

"We're not all close-knit Sicilian families that dine together every night."

"Those big noisy meals keep the generations tight."

"I can't even imagine." Jillian had been raised without an extended family. Her mother's family had cut her off after she married Jillian's father against their wishes. Her father had been an only son and he'd left home at eighteen to make his fortune in the big city. He'd never bothered to introduce his wife and or children to his parents, even though they only lived six hours south of Detroit. "I don't even know if I have cousins and I've never met my grandparents."

"Are they still alive?"

"I don't know." She made a small sound, a hiccup of laughter tinged by frustration. "I believe both my grandmothers and one of my grandfathers might still be alive, but they were never part of our life."

"Why not?"

She smiled up at Vitt's kitchen staff for refilling her coffee. "I don't know for sure but I think my father had a big ego and far too much pride. I think my mother, having lost her parents when she married my father against their wishes, was terrified of losing my father so she supported him on everything, which meant we didn't see grandparents, we didn't do big family holidays. It was always just us, the four of us, Mom, Dad, Katie and me."

"Where does she live?"

"She's…she's—" Jillian broke off, looked away, unable to finish the thought. *Gone*. Katie's gone. Everything in Jillian's life seemed to be about the past. Past tense. Past self. Past life. What she needed was new. What she needed was a future. "Dead. She died. A couple years ago. Katie was only twenty-one."

"I'm sorry."

She looked at him, the pain in her eyes giving away far more than she knew. "I am, too."

Vittorio watched Jill's expression as she talked about her family. Emotions flickered over her face and yet the expression in her eyes never changed. Her eyes revealed grief. Total loss.

"I do think we need to make an effort to include your parents in our wedding. If we set the ceremony for a week from today—next Saturday—we should have plenty of time to invite them and arrange their travel," he said. "Should we place a call to them before dinner? We can make it a conference call, get everyone on the line."

She took a quick sip from her coffee cup. "I don't know if they'll be around. They might be away...traveling."

"I thought you said they didn't like to travel."

"They don't like to fly. Or travel far."

He smiled at her kindly. "You seem nervous. Why would you be nervous?"

"I'm not. I'm just..." she struggled to smile with quivering lips "...overwhelmed. Weddings and castles and change. There's just been a lot of change, Vittorio. I confess, my head is spinning."

"I think you just need something to focus on, like picking out flowers and cake and a bridal gown for the ceremony. My mother is handling the guest list. I will take care of the dinner. You just need to select your gown, music, favorite colors, that sort of thing."

She'd been the one to suggest a formal wedding. She'd been the one to say they needed something public to cement their relationship but suddenly it all seemed very risky. "We're not thinking a big wedding, are we? Just something small, intimate and elegant?"

"I might be wrong, but I believe the guest list has gotten rather extensive. Since Catania is a small place, everyone knows everyone and it was hard for my mother to limit the guest list. But we can try to keep the church ceremony small and invite everyone else to the party after."

Jillian felt increasingly queasy as he talked. Why had she suggested another ceremony? Why hadn't she realized that it could end up big, which would end up attracting a great deal of attention? "Perhaps we should postpone the ceremony a little longer, give us more time to plan."

"With everyone pitching in, a week will give us more than enough time—" He broke off as his mother approached and got to his feet to pull a chair out for her at the table. "Good morning, Mother," he said, dropping a kiss on her cheek. "You have perfect timing. We were just talking about the plans for next Saturday."

"Have you told her about the appointments with the designers?" Theresa asked him, dropping into a chair at the table and crossing one leg over the other. This morning Theresa wore an ivory pantsuit with gold buttons and delicate chains. Her heels were very high, accenting her fashionably slim figure.

"I haven't heard yet," Jillian said, with a glance down at her own uninspiring navy slacks and navy-and-cream striped top. She felt so dowdy next to Vitt's mother, and knew it really was time for a wardrobe update. Less matronly clothes. More stylish and form-fitting.

"You will be meeting with three of our top Italian designers later," Theresa said smoothly. "One arrived last night, two are flying in from Milan this morning. They will each meet with you for a half hour and then work up a design. Each designer will have a sketch to show you before they leave tomorrow. You get to select your favorite gown and then the winning design will be made this week in time for the ceremony next Saturday."

Jillian's eyes grew round. "That sounds incredibly extravagant."

"It's an extravagant ceremony," Theresa replied sharply, "but that's what I understood you wanted."

Jillian turned to Vittorio. "I didn't say I wanted an expensive wedding. And I certainly don't need three different designers flying in to work up three different designs for me to choose from. One designer would have been more than sufficient!"

He shrugged. "You did say you wanted a beautiful dress."

"Yes, but even an off-the-rack gown can be beautiful."

"Because you buy your clothes off the rack," Theresa

said with a sniff. "If you wore couture, you'd know the difference."

"But I don't, and I'm grateful everyone is trying to make the wedding special, but simple is good. Simple can be lovely." Jillian extended a hand toward Vitt. "We can do simple, can't we?"

"It's your wedding," he said, pushing his chair back and getting to his feet. "You're free to do whatever you want."

"I thought it was our wedding," she countered, watching as he ruffled Joe's dark hair, a gentleness in Vitt's eyes as he looked at his son.

She'd never seen that expression before. So much tenderness. A look of pure protection.

He really loved Joe, she realized. He truly wanted to be a father.

"It is our wedding," he answered, "but it's supposed to be your dream wedding. I don't care about the particulars as long as you, me and the priest are there."

Joe was looking up at Vitt now, a gummy smile lighting up his face. Vitt glanced down, caught Joe's cherubic smile and grinned. "Let me change that to you, me, Joseph and the priest," Vitt amended, touching Joe's cheek before walking away.

Jillian watched Vittorio's back for a moment before realizing Theresa was closely watching her. Blushing faintly beneath her mother-in-law's scrutiny, Jillian sat taller and turned to face her. "Thank you for your help in arranging everything. I do appreciate it."

"It was all Vittorio's doing," Theresa answered with a careless wave of her hand. "I told him the designers in Catania would do but he has his own ideas. Always has."

Jillian didn't know what to say to that and rose to get Joe from his high chair.

"So what do you think of the house?" Theresa asked, clearly determined to fill the silence.

"You have a beautiful home," Jillian said, sitting down again with Joe on her lap.

"It's Vittorio's home. He's just kind enough to allow us to live in one of the wings here."

"But I thought the castle had been in the family for nearly a hundred years?"

"It had." Theresa paused, lips pursed a moment as she chose her words. "My husband experienced a reversal of fortune fifteen years ago. We lost everything, including this place. Vittorio dropped out of university to take a job to help us out. He worked very, very hard. There were a lot of problems and a lot of debt. But six years ago he was able to buy the castle back, along with that beautiful villa in Bellagio."

Jillian glanced around the sunlight-dappled terrace with the pots of white roses and lavender wisteria. "I had no idea."

Theresa shrugged. "Vittorio would never tell you something like that. He never takes credit for any of the good things he does—and he does many. But that's how his father is, too. My husband, Salvatore, never thinks of himself. His family has always come first."

"It sounds as if you've had a good marriage."

For the first time since meeting her Theresa genuinely smiled. "I couldn't live without him." And on that note, she got to her feet and headed back into the house.

Jillian spent some time with Joe, and then when he went down for his morning nap, she met with the first of the three fashion designers.

One of the designers was a woman, the other two were men, and all three were so excessively polite that Jillian wondered what they'd been told by Vittorio.

Each designer took measurements. Two asked her questions about what she'd like in a bridal gown, while the third, one of the men, said he had the perfect design in mind and he'd show her later once he'd completed the sketch.

While the three designers retreated to various wings of the castle, Jillian was summoned to the castle's large modern kitchen finished in white marble and commercial-grade stainless steel appliances, to meet with a famous pastry chef from New York flown out just to make the wedding cake. The chef had brought samples of six different cake flavors, along with various icings and fillings.

Jillian sampled bite after bite and narrowed the selection down to three—white chocolate cake with a raspberry filling, a butter cake with lemon cream, and chocolate cake with chocolate mousse—but then didn't want to make the final decision without input from Vittorio. But he'd gone out for the day.

The chef suggested they use all three combinations with each layer of the cake being unique. Jillian agreed and left it to the chef to come up with the overall design.

"Traditional, unusual, colorful, classic, architectural?" the chef asked, trying to swiftly understand Jillian's personal style and vision for the wedding.

"I don't know," she confessed. "I hadn't planned on a big wedding, but it's turning out to be quite formal, so I suppose the cake should be classic. Elegant. Vittorio is very sophisticated. He has tremendous style. I think the cake should at least reflect that."

The pastry chef scribbled some notes, showed Jillian a book of photographs showing elaborately decorated cakes in all kinds of colors, shapes and tiers. They were all beautiful, Jillian told him, and she'd be happy with any of them.

While Jillian was still poring over the photo album, Theresa entered the castle's spacious kitchen to let Jillian know the florist was waiting in the dining room to discuss flowers for the wedding and dinner.

Jillian, who'd felt so unsure of herself during the cake tasting, felt far more comfortable talking with the florist. She'd worked with many florists over the years during her career in the hospitality industry and with a little guidance from the florist, quickly chose a theme of fragrant white gardenias, creamy white roses, contrasted by the silver-gray stems of lamb's ear for softness and texture. The florist suggested weaving in some delicate silver beads for a hint of sheen in the table arrangements, and then for Jillian's bouquet, the florist thought the long stems should be tied with a pale silver satin ribbon for a little extra sophistication.

Jillian loved the idea, and could suddenly see the wedding she wanted—charcoal, black and ivory colors—with lots of candlelight and glamour.

Jillian dragged the florist back to the kitchen where the pastry chef had just finished packing up his dishes and samples and photo albums. She introduced the florist to the chef so they could compare notes, which was perfect since Theresa appeared to announce that the designers were ready to meet with her and she needed to come immediately.

As Jillian and Theresa climbed the stairs to return to the sunny sitting room on the second floor, Theresa warned Jillian not to make any decisions on the different designs until she'd seen all the sketches. "You could easily change your mind several times, so study each design and think about what you want, because this is your day."

They'd paused outside the sitting room with its pale blue walls and white linen-upholstered furniture. "Thank you," Jillian said warmly. "You've done so much for me. I can't even express my gratitude—"

"It's him," Theresa said bluntly. "This is what Vittorio wants for you, and so I support him and am trying to arrange a beautiful wedding and ceremony. But you, I don't know you, and I don't know why you've kept Vittorio from his son for the past year, but no one has asked my opinion, nor will Vittorio ever. He is a man, and he makes his own decisions, and I appreciate that. However, let me give you a little motherly advice. Do not disrespect Vittorio, and do not disrespect this family, because it will not be tolerated. Indiscretions will not be forgiven, either. As Vittorio's wife, you are to bring honor and respect to the family. And if you can't do that, you have no business being here. Do you understand?"

The warmth inside Jillian faded, leaving her chilled. She stiffly nodded her head. "Yes."

"Good," Theresa said more lightly. "Now let's have a look at the bridal gown designs and see which one you prefer."

Jillian spent the next hour dutifully studying the sketches and talking to the designers, but her heart was no longer in it. For a brief moment she'd gotten excited about the wedding. For a brief moment while consulting with the florist she'd felt like a real bride making real decisions about her dream wedding, but Theresa's stern warning outside the sitting room had brought Jillian crashing back to earth.

This was not a normal wedding. Their ceremony next Saturday was not going to be a happy day.

With a heavy heart, Jillian gazed at each of the three sketches again—one dress looked like a princess ball gown with layers and layers of tulle and delicate pearl beading, another looked like a fitted ivory satin negligee with a daringly low back and snug shoulder straps, and the third was a slim empire-style dress made of white chiffon, topped with a jeweled bodice and a matching Cleopatra-style jeweled collar.

All three bridal gowns were stunning, all three were glamorous and all three would cost a fortune.

"They're all beautiful," Jillian said, going from one to the other and around again without making a decision. "I could wear any one of them."

"Yes, dear, but you can only have one, and the designers

need to go home and get to work," Theresa said coolly. "So which gown is it to be?"

Jillian lightly ran her fingertips over the sketch in her hand. It was the ball gown sketch, the one that looked most like the kind of dress Cinderella would have worn the night she met the prince.

The first night Jillian had gone to dinner with Vitt she'd thought him a prince.

That first night she'd been so sure there would be happily-ever-after.

She set aside the ball gown design to look at the satin 1930s glamour gown. The dress looked like something a rich man would have his mistress wear. It spoke of sex and seduction and money.

And then there was the chiffon empire-style dress with the jeweled bodice and collar. The embroidery and jewels looked modern and yet the chiffon added softness, making her think of the silvery fuzzy lamb's ear leaves tucked among the fragrant white flower blossoms.

These three gowns were all so fancy, so showy, she couldn't actually imagine wearing any of them.

Yet she couldn't say that to the designers. She couldn't hurt their feelings.

She flipped through the female fashion designer's sketch-book, pausing briefly at a sketch she hadn't been shown. It was a strapless ivory silk gown with a full ruched silk skirt without any embellishment other than a sage green satin ribbon at the waist. The green satin ribbon had been tied into a soft bow and the ends dangled all the way to the skirt's hem.

It was simple, maybe too simple, which is why Jillian hadn't been shown it, but she loved the color green, and the ruched ball skirt with the organza overlay.

"I like that one best," a deep male voice, a very calm voice, said from behind her shoulder. "It looks like you."

She glanced over her shoulder at Vittorio, tears shimmering in her eyes. "You think so?"

He nodded and reached out to catch one of the tears before it fell. "Why are you sad?"

"She's not sad," Theresa said sharply, "and you're not supposed to be here. The gown is supposed to be kept secret—"

"We're already married, Mother. This is a renewal of vows for the benefit of our family." He leaned over the back of the couch, took the sketchpad with the color drawing of the ivory gown and green ribbon and held it up. "Who did this one?"

The female designer raised her hand. "It's mine."

"This is the one Jill wants," Vitt told her. He nodded to the other designers. "Thank you for coming today. As promised, you will be well compensated for the consultation. Thank you everyone, and now we must say goodbye as Jill and I have someplace we have to be."

Jillian lifted her head, met Vitt's gaze. He nodded slightly. She rose and together they left the room.

"Where are we going?" she murmured as they started down the stairs.

"Out. Away. I thought we could both use some air, and time to ourselves." He glanced down at her as they reached the bottom stair. "Would you like that?"

"Very much."

"Good. So would I."

CHAPTER NINE

VITTORIO opened the front door to the front steps and sunshine flooded the stone entry. The air felt fresh, the sky was blue with just a few wispy clouds, and a cream two-seater convertible sports car gleamed in the circular driveway.

"That's a beautiful car," she said, descending the steps to examine the car's flowing lines from the curving panoramic windshield to the sleek rear end. "Has to be a 1950s design," she added.

"Good eye. 1955," he said, smiling at her. "A Lancia Aurelia."

"Don't they call these B24 Spiders?"

Vittorio laughed softly as he opened the passenger door for her. "They do. How did you know?"

She glanced admiringly into the interior with its dark red leather seats and dash. "My dad loved cars. He was always buying new cars and living in Detroit—" She broke off, horrified by what she'd just revealed and then panicked, she babbled on as she slid into the passenger seat. "Dad still watches car auctions on TV."

Vittorio closed the door behind her and moved to the driver's seat. "You never mentioned your father's interest at Bellagio."

She glanced up at the chiseled features of his face to see if he'd caught her slip, but Vittorio looked relaxed, his expression almost happy. "I didn't realize you liked old cars, too," she said, thinking that her mention of Detroit hadn't registered, "because all of your cars at the lake villa were new."

"And what do you prefer?" he asked, closing his door.

"I do love classic cars best."

"Sounds like you are your father's daughter," he said, starting the car.

Jillian grew hot, her skin prickly. She'd definitely been her father's daughter the first twelve years of her life. She'd loved his energy and charm and ready laugh. "Growing up I was very close to him," she said quietly. "I was proud of being a Daddy's girl."

"What changed?" Vittorio asked, shifting gears and heading down the driveway to the castle's impressive gates.

She was silent a long moment as Vittorio pulled away from the Normandy castle with its turret and tower to head down the drive toward town.

The sun shone brightly and Jillian lifted a hand to shield her eyes. "His job," she said at length. "He had problems at work."

"What sort of problems?" Vitt asked, sliding on a pair of sunglasses.

"Financial."

Vitt shot her a glance. "Did he embezzle money?"

"No. At least, I don't think so. We never talked about it at home. My father wasn't open and my mother didn't ask questions. They had a very traditional marriage. Dad was the head of the family and made all the decisions. It was Mom's job to agree with him."

Vitt shot her a brief glance. "You're nothing like your mother."

She laughed despite herself. "No, I'm not. Maybe that's why we're not close." But then her smile disappeared as she thought of her sister, a beautiful brunette who'd taken after their mother. Mom and Katie had been close, practically been best friends. "My sister and Mom talked every single day though, sometimes three or four times a day. Even when Katie was at college she called Mom to get her advice, ask her opinion. I used to tell Katie to grow up, become independent but she said Mom needed her, and now, looking back, I realize Katie was probably right. Mom hasn't had much of a life."

"When is the last time you saw them then? Your sister's funeral?"

Jillian dug her nails into her hands and looked away. "I wasn't able to make the funeral."

"What?"

She felt Vitt's stare and she lifted her shoulders. "I was in Switzerland working. There was no graveside service. Mom and Dad just took Katie's ashes home."

"That's just strange."

"As I said, we're not close." She turned to look at him, eyes huge in her pale face. "I haven't seen them since I graduated from college, and that was five years ago."

"Don't you want to see them?"

"Yes." Her voice broke. She swallowed hard. "But there are reasons we don't get together, and I have to respect those reasons." Jillian grabbed her long hair in her hand to keep it from blowing in her face. "I'm not saying it's easy, because it's not. I wanted to go home and see them after Katie's death. I wanted to be with the people who loved Katie as much as I did, but I couldn't go, and I grieved on my own, and it was horrible." She blinked back tears. "But then I changed jobs and moved from Zurich to Istanbul and that helped. Helped distract me from always thinking about losing Katie."

Vittorio glanced at her again, his sunglasses hiding his eyes and yet from the set of his mouth she knew he was thinking over every word she'd said.

She'd said a lot, too.

"Can we talk about something else?" she said huskily. "Talking about my family just makes me miss Katie even more."

They drove along the lower slopes of Mount Etna, passing through acres of black lava only to arrive at terraced fields of vineyards and almond and hazelnut groves.

They stopped at Roman ruins an hour and a half outside Paterno and Vittorio held her hand as they walked down stone stairs cut from the hillside to the bottom of what once must have been a very grand amphitheater. In places the rows of stone seats climbed perfectly up the grassy hillside. In other areas the stones had been broken and toppled and lay in pieces on the ground.

"Can you imagine attending a play or a concert here?" Jillian asked, doing a slow circle to fully savor the amphitheater's grandeur.

"Now and then concerts are still performed here. It doesn't happen often anymore—the last time was ten years ago—but it's a magical thing to have the theatre come alive, with all the performers lit by moonlight and candlelight."

Jillian sat down on a stone bench that was still largely intact. "We're in a field with a secret Roman amphitheater that's just an hour from your home. I'm jealous!"

"It is beautiful. And the amazing thing is, we have ruins like this all over Sicily. Every couple of miles you'll find the tumbled stones of a Doric temple, Byzantine church, Norman castle, Greek and Roman amphitheaters. But the ruins aren't merely in the countryside. Our cities are filled with ancient gates and bridges, tombs and altars. We have two thousand years of history on this island, and it's all created the strong, modern Sicilian character."

"You're proud to be Sicilian," she said, looking up at him.

Vittorio nodded. "Very proud. Sicilians haven't just been

shaped by thousands of years of different cultures and rulers, but also by the land and weather. Here in Sicily we have six months of perfect warm weather followed by months of torrential rains. The interior of the island is dry, rocky and arid, while our exterior is one of endless coastlines with picturesque beach towns and breathtaking views. We're surrounded by water and yet at the center is our Mount Etna, Europe's largest, most active volcano."

"A place of extremes," she said.

"Exactly so," he agreed, extending a hand to her. "Shall we go so I can show you more?"

They stopped in Bronte, enjoying a simple meal in the restaurant's charming, shady courtyard before Vittorio ducked into a boutique and emerged with a silk scarf and pair of sunglasses. "For your hair," he said, tying the scarf under her chin. "And your eyes," he added, slipping the sunglasses onto her nose.

Touched by his thoughtful gesture, she rose on tiptoe and kissed him. "Thank you."

He gazed down at her for a long moment, a small muscle pulling in his jaw. "My pleasure."

And then they were climbing into the Lancia sports car and heading to Paterno. Riding home in the sleek two-seater convertible, Jillian felt very chic in her sunglasses and scarf. "This was a really nice afternoon," she commented as he slowed to allow a shepherd and his flock of sheep to cross the road.

"It still is," he agreed, dark eyes holding hers, before focusing again on the road. As he drove they sat in silence, mellowed by their meal, the warmth of the sun and the scenic drive.

It wasn't until they were on the outskirts of Paterno that Vittorio spoke again. "I want to call your parents when we return and personally invite them to the wedding. I will let them know that I can handle all arrangements, and have a plane at their disposal—"

"Vitt, not this again!"

"Jill, you are their only daughter."

"Maybe, but they won't come. They just won't."

He shot her a swift glance. "How do you know if you haven't asked them?"

"Because I know them!"

"But I don't, and if we're to be a family, I want to know them, and I'd think they'd want to get to know me."

"They don't. It sounds dreadful put like that, but it's the truth. They don't want to know anyone anymore, not after Katie's boyfriend—" She broke off, bit down hard into her lip, astonished that she would once again say so much.

He shot her a swift glance. "What did Katie's boyfriend do?"

Jillian closed her eyes, hating herself.

"Jill?" he demanded.

She looked at him, expression stricken. "Marco hurt her."

"*He* was the one that killed her?"

"Yes." She ducked her head, studied her laced fingers, remembered how when she and Katie were young they'd hold hands when they crossed the street. Held hands when Katie got scared. Tears burned her eyes, but they were nothing compared to the emotion tearing up her heart. "So now my parents don't go anywhere or meet anyone. They just live in their little house in Fort Lauderdale and soak up the sun and maybe play a round of golf."

For a moment Vittorio said nothing and then he spoke quietly, flatly. "I am not Marco. I would never hurt you, or your family—"

"That may be, but we will not call them. I will not call them."

"Then I will." He glanced at her. "I have their number, Jill. Home and cellular."

She turned her face away from him, jaw set. He didn't know. He didn't understand. "Don't do it, Vitt. It's not a good idea. You *have* to trust me on this one."

"Like you trust me?" he retorted.

She stiffened, her spine rigid.

"Your parents are important," he added. "They're not just your parents, but they're Joseph's grandparents and they should be part of his life."

"But I don't want them in Joe's life! He's not safe with them in his life. Leave them in Florida. It's where they belong."

"How can you be so bitter?"

"Because you don't know what my father put us through!"

"What did he put you through?"

"Hell." Then she smiled bitterly to hide the hot lance of pain. It had been hell, too. Her childhood had been so happy that she hadn't even been prepared for the terrible things that happened when she turned twelve. Couldn't have imagined that she'd be ripped from that idyllic, sheltered childhood and thrust into a world of constant fear. To know that your father was a hated and hunted man…to live believing your family was in constant danger…to go to bed every night thinking it might be your last…

"Your teeth are chattering," Vitt said.

They were, too, but that's because she was freezing. "I'm cold."

"It's eighty-four degrees out."

"So?"

"You're not cold. You're afraid."

"Why would I be afraid?"

Vitt abruptly pulled over to the side of the road and shifted into Park. Unbuckling his seat belt he turned all the way in his seat, his body angled forward to face her. "You're afraid because if I call your parents, it will reveal all your secrets and all your lies—"

"I have no secrets!"

His jaw flexed. His nostrils flared. He looked as if he was barely keeping his temper in check. "You have one hour to make that call, or I will."

Vittorio shifted into Drive and steered the Lancia Aurelia back onto the highway.

Jillian sat with her hands clenched in her lap. For a moment she felt nothing. Not even panic. And then slowly her head filled with noise, a buzzing sound that became a roar.

He'd found something out. Something important. Otherwise why would he want to call her parents personally? Why would he be so determined to speak to them, introduce himself, meet them personally?

Instinct and self-preservation told her that this wasn't a courtesy call. This phone call had nothing to do with playing the gracious bridegroom. He was cementing his power.

He was ensuring security.

He was going after the truth. And he was going after the truth because he didn't trust her.

Smart man, she thought, swallowing around the lump in her throat.

Blinking back hot tears, she stared blindly out the car onto the fields dotted with stone walls as they drove the rest of the distance in agonizing silence.

Pulling up before the castle, Vittorio shifted into Park even as Jillian was throwing open the car door and jumping out. "You're down to forty minutes, Jill. You have forty minutes to decide what you want to do. I'll be in the library waiting for you."

"I've nothing to tell you!"

"That's a shame. Because you have so much to lose."

Jillian turned and ran up the steps into the house, and didn't stop running until she'd reached the nursery where Joe was sleeping.

Maria put a finger to her lips when Jillian burst into the room. The shades were down, darkening the room and Jillian nodded as she continued to the crib. She had to see Joe, had to see him as only then could she believe everything would be okay.

Jillian stared down at him, taking in his flushed cheeks and his rosy lips. He'd never looked more angelic. "Did he have a good day?" she whispered to Maria.

"Yes. He played and played and he ate a lot and we also went for walks."

Jillian's chest squeezed. She longed to reach out and touch him but she didn't dare wake him. Instead she smiled at Maria and went to her room, where she changed from her navy striped top and slacks into a simple white linen dress. She ran a comb through her hair and then turned away from the mirror. Don't be scared, she told herself, heading for the stairs.

Reaching the library on the second floor, Jillian wiped her now damp palms on the sides of her dress before opening the library door. "What do you want to know?" she asked.

"Everything," he said as she stepped into the room.

She closed the door behind her before approaching his desk where he'd been typing something on his laptop computer. "But you know everything."

"Do I, *Jill*?"

"Yes. I have no secrets. My dad's a jerk. My mom's weak. My sister's dead. What else is there?"

"Then who, *cara*, is Anne? And Carol? And Lee?" He caught her expression and smiled grimly. "Yes, my wife of many identities. Who are you really?"

"How long have you known about the different identities?"

"Since yesterday. But I had suspicions before."

She nodded. "Then you know everything…"

"I don't know why, and I don't know who you were before you went into the government's witness protection program, but I have my suspicions."

Jillian startled and he nodded. "I'd wager this castle that your father is linked to organized crime," Vitt continued, "and I'd bet my Lancia that he's a mob boss from Detroit, a man who confessed everything he knew to the FBI to save himself from going to prison."

He smiled and gestured to the phone. "Now I just need you to confirm it for me."

She swayed on her feet. "I can't, Vitt."

"Can't or won't?"

"Both."

"Then I will, and once I call them, and let them know you're here with me, I'm confident they'll tell me what I need to know—"

"They won't."

"Not even if they think you're in trouble?"

She laughed. "God, no! They didn't when Marco kidnapped Katie, so why would they do it for me?"

"Is that how your sister died?"

She made a low tormented sound. "The tragic thing is that they didn't even want Katie. They wanted my father. But my father wouldn't dream of sacrificing himself for anyone else, much less his daughter."

"And so she died."

"In a car bomb. Can you believe that? She thought she was free to go. She thought she'd escaped the danger. Instead they blew her up as she started her car." Jillian dragged her fist across her face, rubbing away tears before they fell. "The police called it an accident. But everyone on the inside knew it wasn't an accident. And so the government stepped in and Mom and Dad were moved to yet another location. I didn't change my name, but I did change jobs, going from Switzerland to Turkey."

"And it was in Turkey you met me."

She nodded. "I thought you were perfect for me, too. Until I discovered who you were. So I ran. Just as I've been running for my life ever since I was twelve."

He rose from behind his desk and went to her, caught her hands in his and drew her toward him. "You don't have to be afraid—not here, not anymore."

"I wish I could believe that. I really do."

"Why can't you?"

"Because bad things happen when we let our guard down. Katie let her guard down—"

"You're not Katie," he interrupted, lifting her hand with her wedding ring to his mouth and kissing her ring finger and then her palm. "You will never be Katie, and I promise that nothing will happen to you if you trust me. I can protect you. And my family will protect you. Always."

Her gaze clung to his. She wanted to believe him, she really did, because she needed to believe in someone, needed to believe the world could be a good place, and a safe place. Her world had often felt very dark and harsh and cold and yet whenever she was with Vitt, she felt warm.

She felt safe.

"Kiss me," she whispered. "Kiss me and make all these bad feelings go away."

"That's the smartest thing I've heard you say all day," he murmured, lifting her face to cover her mouth with his. He kissed her slowly, deeply, lips drawing from hers an immediate and almost feverish response.

She needed him.

She needed him desperately.

For the longest time she'd felt as if she was drowning but

maybe he could save her. Maybe he was strong enough, smart enough…

Hope blazed to life. Hope and heat kindling into hot desire.

With his mouth on hers, Vittorio walked her backward across the library until she felt the dark paneled door against her hips.

He leaned past her, turned the lock on the door, and then moved closer, his tall, lithe, firm body pressing into her.

She loved the feel of his body against her and the warm hard ridge of his erection rubbing against her inner thighs. She wanted him and she groaned against his mouth.

"Careful, *cara*, or I will take you here," he warned, teeth nipping at her soft, swollen lower lip.

"Good," she answered, her body trembling with need.

"Don't tempt me," he said, his warm breath caressing her skin as his lips brushed the curve of her ear and then lower to the tender hollow below. "Because I'm dangerously close to losing control."

She turned so that her lips brushed his. "Lose it."

"Don't say that. You don't know how I feel. I'm angry, Jill, I'm angry and frustrated and I don't want to hurt you—"

"I'm not afraid of a little pain."

"Stop it," he growled. "Don't talk that way."

"Then take me and make me forget everything but you and me and being here together right now."

"I cannot fight you, and me." He tugged the hem of her white linen dress toward her hips and put his hand between her legs. "But don't say I didn't warn you."

Jillian felt as though she'd burst into fire on the inside. Her body felt wild. Her nerves explosive. She arched against Vittorio, demanding more.

He stroked over her cream silk panty, stroking the soft feminine shape of her.

She gasped and tipped her head against the door, giving herself over to exquisite sensation as hot, silvery shots of electricity burst through her, tightening her nipples and melting her core.

He lifted the edge of the panty, moving beneath the thin satin band to slide his fingers beneath the fabric, to run his fingers against her, then between the folds to the softest, warmest part of her. His fingers felt slick against her, which meant she was wet. Very wet.

Her mouth dried as he rubbed her between two fingers and she rocked helplessly against his hand, responding with not just her body, but also her heart.

With him she was safe. With him she was home. There could never be any other place she belonged but with him.

"You're mine," he ground out, his voice husky in her ear. "And I'm going to fill you and make you mine, and you will always be mine."

"Yes." Because of course she was his. She'd always been his. It was inevitable from the very first meeting in the hotel lobby. Fate brought them together, and it was up to fate to keep them together.

She heard him unzip his trousers as he freed himself, and then with one hand he pressed the head of his hot, hard erection against the wet entrance to her body.

He teased her for a moment with the tip, rubbing it across her wetness, and then up and down over her softness until she panted with need. And once she moaned his name, he plunged inside of her, filling her all the way.

She sucked in air, and held it bottled in her lungs as her heart seemed to burst open inside of her.

She loved him.

She did.

He and Joe were everything. Life, breath, hope. She circled

his neck with her arms, pressed her lips to his. "I need you forever," she whispered.

"You have me forever," he answered.

Tears burned her eyes. "Promise."

"I promise."

"No matter what?"

"No matter what." He lifted her against the wall, hooking her leg over his arm to thrust into her even deeper, stretching her, filling her, making her one with him.

She gasped at the fullness of them together, overwhelmed by the warmth and the dizzying emotions and intense sensation. He thrust into her again and again, and with each thrust she knew he was making her his.

But then he'd known from the very beginning that she needed this hard, physical coupling to feel loved.

Making love with Vittorio always made her feel loved, but she needed it now more than ever when everything felt so unpredictable, when their connection felt so fragile.

She buried her fingers in his cool, crisp hair, pressed her face to his neck, her lips to his warm fragrant skin, aware of each long, measured stroke of him taking her, filling her. With each thrust he edged her closer and closer to that point of no return, pushing her past reason and control until she shattered in a thousand pieces. He climaxed as she came, and dipping his head he covered her mouth with his, swallowing her scream in a kiss.

CHAPTER TEN

WITH one arm still braced against the wall, Vittorio slowly withdrew, and struggled to catch his breath as Jill slid down the door to sit in a boneless heap on the floor.

Tucking himself back into his trousers, he drew up the zipper knowing his body had found release but his emotions were tangled, pleasure diminished by sorrow.

She'd been through so much. She'd lived through chaos and betrayal, grief and pain.

Her pain hurt him. He should have comforted her, not taken her savagely against the wall.

He understood why she used sex as a paste or plaster to smooth problems over, but why did he? He knew sex solved nothing. Sex just masked problems until they revealed themselves again.

Dark, wrenching emotion filled him as he glanced down at her. She sat on the floor and leaned against the dark paneled door. Her thick blond hair tumbled over her shoulders in disheveled curls, her white linen dress was creased around her slim hips, and her long bare legs stretched before her making her look fragile and so very vulnerable.

Because she was vulnerable. Heartbreakingly vulnerable. And now that he understood her secrets and pain, he wondered how she'd endured it. How she could lose so much—family, friends, home—and yet be so strong. So determined to make a good life for their son.

His lingering frustration morphed into admiration. She was such a fighter. Such a complex woman. Intelligent, sensual, mysterious, stubborn. Very, very stubborn.

His chest tightened as his gaze met hers. She looked up at him with enormous eyes. Whether she had brown eyes, or blue eyes, pink or purple, it didn't matter. They were beautiful. She was beautiful. And he had never wanted her more.

Or needed to protect her more.

She did need him, too. He understood that now. She needed him not just for protection, but love, and patience and compassion. Jill was battered and bruised from fourteen years of fear and intimidation. It would take time for her to learn to trust people again. Hopefully she could trust him.

Hopefully she understood that she was safe with him. Hopefully she understood that here in Paterno she was finally safe. Home.

Crouching next to her, he buried his hand in her tangled curls and gently lifted her face to his. Her eyes shone, glimmering with tears.

"Don't cry, *cara*. No one will hurt you ever again. I promise you that," he said huskily, angered that her father had failed to protect his daughters, angered that the government had failed to protect her sister. "I will protect you. I will always protect you."

Emotion darkened her eyes. "But you don't even know who I am."

He stared deep into her eyes, looking so intently that he felt as if he could see the shy little girl inside the woman. "You are Jillian d'Severano. Joe's mother and my wife."

Her eyes turned liquid and she blinked hard. "Would you feel the same way if you knew my father was Frank Giordano?"

For a moment Vittorio couldn't breathe. His mind darkened. Frank Giordano was the scum of the scum. A man so selfish and self-serving he'd turned on his own organization to keep himself from serving time. "Frankie's your father?"

She nodded and tears clung to her lower lashes. "I'm sorry."

"Not your fault," he said, voice sharper than he intended. He'd wondered these past two days if she was possibly related to Frankie Giordano. He'd hoped, even prayed she wasn't. There was a lot of bad blood between his family and Frank Giordano. Very bad blood. His father would be sick that Vitt had married Frank's daughter.

"You're upset," she whispered, reading his expression.

"You didn't commit any crimes, Jill. You are not responsible for your father."

"But I am." She ground her teeth together. "I am responsible for my family's name, just the way you are responsible for yours. And I know I'm not the kind of person your family would want you to marry. I know they'd be horrified to discover Joe was the grandson of Frank Giordano—"

He cut off her tortured words with a kiss because he couldn't bear to hear more. Because she was right. His family had fought for twenty years to escape the taint of being connected to the mafia, and having the daughter of Detroit's most infamous mob boss be Vittorio's wife wouldn't help the d'Severano reputation, but Vitt had chosen her because he loved her.

He loved her.

The truth exploded within him, searing his mind and heart. He'd loved her all this time. It was love that drove him to search for her after she disappeared without a word from the villa in Bellagio. It was love twisted with pain when he discovered that Jill had given birth to a son.

He knew the child was his.

Just as he'd known from the first time he spotted Jill in the hotel lobby in Istanbul that she was meant for him.

Her lips quivered beneath his and her mouth tasted salty from her tears.

"Shh." He comforted her, his hand cupping her face, caressing her warm flushed cheek. "It's okay. I promise you, everything is okay."

"I will always be a danger to your family," she whispered against his mouth, her voice faint, unsteady.

He drew back to look into her eyes. "You are not a danger—"

"There are bad people out there, Vittorio. Bad people who are determined to find my father."

"Then they'll have to go through me, *cara*, because they cannot have you. They can not touch you. I make that promise to you as a d'Severano, and a d'Severano always keeps his word."

She gazed up at him, torn between hope and concern. "Will your family feel the same way?"

"This is my home. You are my wife. If anyone in my family has a problem with you or your past, they don't need to come here—"

"Vittorio!"

"I mean it. Yes, I've worked hard to restore the d'Severano honor and fortune, and I will never regret the sacrifices I made to take care of my family, but my loyalty is to you, and our son."

Jill reached up to lightly touch his face, her fingers infinitely gentle on his cheek and jaw. "You really mean that?"

"I do." He nodded and rose, and then held a hand out to her to assist Jill to her feet. "And while I don't like keeping secrets from my family, I don't think it's necessary we share your background with everyone at dinner tonight. I'll find a way to break the news, and I will do it soon, but this evening isn't the time."

"I'm meeting the family tonight?"

He nodded, his mouth quirking. "My sisters are having fits that they haven't met you yet, and my father is very eager to meet my wife. It'll be a large group—uncles, aunts, cousins—can you handle that?"

She nodded. "Yes."

"Good." He unlocked the door, started to open it, then stopped. "So what is your real name, since we know it's not really Jill Smith?"

"Alessia," she said softly. "But I haven't been Alessia for fourteen years. I'm Jillian now, and that's who I want to be."

"Then that's who you will be. So go shower and dress and try to relax, because I should warn you, my sisters are a lot like my mother—strong, talkative, rather intense—but hopefully a little more friendly."

Jillian's head spun as she climbed the stairs to their master suite on the third floor. She'd done it, she thought, reaching the bedroom and closing the door.

She'd told him. She'd told him the truth and nothing horrible had happened.

The planets hadn't collided.

No stars had fallen from the sky.

No scary men had jumped out of bushes and snatched her away.

Maybe all the bad things were behind her. Maybe, she thought, stripping off her dress and stepping beneath the showerhead with the faucets turned on full force, just maybe, everything would be okay.

Relief swept through her as the water beat down, first icy, then scalding until she finally adjusted the water to the perfect temperature.

Mind spinning, she soaped up, shampooed her hair and rinsed off all while thinking that her fears seemed so silly now. Why hadn't she trusted Vitt sooner?

Why had she thought he'd be like her father?

How tragic that she hadn't trusted him before. It would have saved them all so much heartache as well as lost time together.

Once dry, Jill styled her hair, then applied makeup, before slipping into the simple black cocktail dress hanging in the closet.

She felt like a different woman as she tugged up the dress's zipper. It was such a relief to have shared the truth with someone. Such a relief to know she wasn't alone. Keeping the secret had been a crushing burden and suddenly she felt lighter. Freer. Happier.

Twisting her hair into a silky chignon she stared at her reflection in the master bathroom's enormous mirror, her brown eyes smiling shyly, her mouth curving uncertainly.

He knew the truth about her, knew she was Frank Giordano's daughter, and he hadn't pulled away in disgust.

But having him just accept the truth wasn't enough. She wanted his love. She wanted his heart.

Yet how could he love her if he didn't know her? She needed him to know her, the real her, the woman who was falling in love with him.

Looking hard at her pale reflection, Jillian took a deep breath and removed one contact lens, and then the other, taking the brown colored lenses out to reveal her natural eye color—a vivid, and rather startling, turquoise green.

Moving to the sink, she washed the brown contact lenses down the drain and then washed her hands, all the while looking at her heart-shaped face with the high cheekbones, aristocratic nose and strong chin.

This is you, she told her reflection, this is you without artifice and make-believe. This is the you Vitt needs to see.

She didn't know how Vitt would react when he saw her eyes had changed color again but at least tonight when he saw her face, he would see her real face. He'd finally see her.

Vittorio rapped on the bathroom door. "My family is gathered downstairs and waiting."

"I'm ready," she said, opening the door and stepping out, wondering how long it'd take him to notice what she'd done.

He tipped his head, studied her. He'd noticed the change immediately. "You look...different."

"Is it my hair? I can take it down."

"It's not your hair."

"Maybe it's the dress. It's a little big."

"Everything in your wardrobe is big."

"I never bought new clothes after I had Joe. But I don't mind. And no one's really going to be looking at me tonight, right?"

He smiled with his eyes. "Keep telling yourself that if it makes you feel better." And then he drew a velvet pouch from his pocket. "But maybe this will add a little sparkle and shine to your black frock."

Shyly she bent her head forward so that he could fasten the elaborate gold clasp at the back of her neck. The choker was snug, the strands heavy with precious stones.

"Turn around," he said.

She did, and for a moment he said nothing and then he tipped her chin up with one finger. "Green eyes tonight."

She nodded.

"How did you know you'd be getting emeralds?" he asked, sounding amused.

"I didn't."

"You just decided to swap out your colored lenses to-night?"

She fingered the precious jewels at her throat. "I decided I was tired of hiding, so I threw away the contacts."

"Your real eye color is green?"

She nodded.

"And what is your real hair color? Red?" he guessed.

"How did you know?"

He'd been smiling but his smile died. "It's the one color you've never been." Vitt reached out to her smooth chignon and touched the twisted strands at her nape. "My wife has red hair and green eyes. How odd to think I've never really known her."

"But you have. This—" and she gestured to her face and body "—this is the real me. The only me. The one you met in Istanbul. The one you took to the villa. The one who had your baby."

"Good. Because you are the one I wanted in Istanbul, and you are the one I loved in Bellagio, and you are the one I want to help raise our son." Then he took her hand in his, kissed her hand, before tucking it in the crook of his arm.

Together they descended the staircase and entered the grand dining room with the pale blue-and-cream frescoes on the walls. Jillian stiffened in the doorway when everyone turned to look at them.

"I know it's a lot of people," Vitt murmured reassuringly, "but just be yourself and everyone will love you."

She nodded, even as she pressed her hand tighter into the crook of his arm.

They hadn't made much progress into the room before two attractive women moved toward them.

"My sisters," Vitt said beneath his breath. "They take after my mother. Just do your best."

"That's not comforting at all," she answered in a whisper.

Vittorio made the introductions. "Bianca and Carlina, I'd like you to meet Jill, my wife. Jill, this is Carlina, the youngest of my sisters, and Bianca, the oldest. Guiliana isn't here. She lives in Europe with her family."

The four of them made small talk for a few minutes before Bianca and Carlina came up with an excuse to get Jillian alone. Knowing his sisters wouldn't be satisfied until they'd had their time with her, he allowed them to drag her off toward a private corner. He in the meantime went to greet his paternal grandmother who was already sitting in her chair at the table.

He stooped to give her a kiss. She was small and rather frail but her mind remained sharp. "Nonna, how are you?" he asked, sitting down in a chair close to hers and taking her hands in his.

"The sun was shining today and I am alive. What could be better?"

Vitt grinned. "Not much, Nonnie."

His grandmother nodded at Jillian, who was still in the corner with his sisters. "How did this happen?"

"The baby?"

She narrowed her eyes. "I know how babies are made. I had nine of them. But how is it we are only meeting your family now?"

He shrugged. "There were problems. We're working them out."

"Good. Children need their mother and father together in one house."

"I agree."

She tipped her head, considering Jillian. "She's Italian, isn't she? Maybe even Sicilian. Look at her nose, the cheekbones, you can see it in her face."

His grandmother was smart. He smiled at her and patted her hand. "Would you like to meet her?"

"Why do you think I'm here?"

Laughing softly, he rose to get Jill, but before he could pry Jill away from his sisters, his mother entered the dining room then, pushing his father's wheelchair.

Vitt hadn't seen his father since arriving home and approached his father right away, bending over the wheelchair to kiss his father on the cheek. "Father, you look well. What have you been doing? Chasing *Madre* around the bedroom?"

His father's dark eyes shone, and his mouth pulled into a smile. "Impudent dog," his father said, his voice distorted by the ventilator helping him breathe.

Vittorio had always admired his father, but one of the things he enjoyed most about his father was his sense of humor. "Everyone tells me I take after you."

Salvatore rolled his eyes before looking toward the corner. "Is that your wife talking to your sisters?"

"Yes."

"Go get her. I'm anxious to meet her."

Jillian startled when Vitt suddenly touched her low on her back. "My father wants to meet you," he said quietly as he drew her away from the others. "He speaks with difficulty, and it's not always easy to understand him, so please be patient," he said, leading her across the room to where his father sat.

Jillian's breath caught in her throat as she spotted the family resemblance between Vitt and his father. Salvatore d'Severano was tall like Vitt, and very broad-shouldered, and while probably once powerfully built, he was now thin, his body stooped, the muscles connecting his large frame slack from years of atrophy.

But while his body appeared frail, his dark eyes burned with a fierce intelligence and his intense gaze seemed to see everything as she approached his wheelchair.

"Did he have a stroke?" she asked, suddenly terribly nervous.

"No. He was shot. It left him paralyzed."

"He's a quadriplegic?"

"Yes."

And then they'd arrived at Salvatore's side and Vittorio again made the introductions. "Father, this is my wife, Jill. Jill, this is my father, Salvatore d'Severano."

"Hello, Mr. d'Severano," she said. "It's a pleasure to meet you."

"There's no mister here," he answered gruffly. "You are my daughter now. Welcome to the family."

"Thank you." Her voice was pitched low. "That means a great deal to me."

He looked at her with dark searching eyes. "If you are happy, why do you cry?"

"I'm not crying," she denied, blinking hard to keep her eyes dry.

"Has my son made you so very unhappy?"

"No."

"I may be paralyzed, but I'm no fool."

"I promise you, it's not Vitt. He's been very good considering...considering..."

"Considering all the drama?" Salvatore finished for her, eyes watering with the effort it cost him to speak.

She nodded.

His brow furrowed. "You look so very familiar. I can't help but think I know you."

She shook her head. "I would have remembered you."

"Perhaps I know your family. You are Sicilian, aren't you?"

"No. American."

"Yes, but your family is Italian, from Sicily, I am sure of it."

Again Jillian shook her head but then her composure cracked and murmuring excuses, she slipped from the room, ushing past everyone to push through the hall door to the outside terrace. It was a quiet night, the terrace lit by just the moon. Jillian paced back and forth before leaning against the stone balustrade to draw great gasps of air into her lungs.

Of course her family was Italian, and she still took pride in her Italian heritage. But her father...

She was so ashamed of her father. And so disgusted, too.

He'd sacrificed Katie to save his own skin. How could he do that to her? How could he do that to all of them?

What kind of monster was he?

"What did my father say?" Vittorio asked quietly from behind her, his footsteps so silent she hadn't even heard him approach.

She shook her head. "Nothing."

"Then why are you so upset?"

She turned to face him. "He was so kind to me, but he wouldn't be if he knew who my father was."

"He probably wouldn't like who your father was, but he wouldn't hold it against you, *cara*. My father is a bigger man than that."

"How did he get hurt?"

Vittorio leaned against the balustrade next to her. "He decided to leave the mafia."

"So they shot him?"

"Yes."

"How old were you when it happened?"

"Seventeen."

"Just a teenager!"

"Yes."

She heard something in his voice that made her look closely at him and she saw the shadow of grief in his eyes. "It must have been terrible for you."

"It was."

She waited for him to say more, hoped he'd say more

because she so badly wanted to understand him, but he didn't.

Instead he straightened, and held out a hand to her. "Come *cara*, let's return to the house, join the others again. Tonight is supposed to be a celebration, a chance to welcome you into the family. There will be plenty of opportunities to talk about the past, but tonight is about the present and our plans for the future."

Hand in hand they returned to the dining room where everyone was just taking their places at the long tables. Jillian was disappointed to discover that she and Vittorio would now be sitting next to each other but across the large square table from each other.

But Vittorio did not neglect her during the lengthy meal. Instead she felt his eyes on her time and again, and more than once she felt as though he was seducing her with his warm gaze, using his dizzying physical presence to arouse her, weaken her, make her want him.

He didn't realize she always wanted him.

He didn't realize she would always want him as she'd fallen in love with him. Hopelessly in love.

While the family talked, switching easily between Italian Sicilian and English for Jillian's benefit, she tried to imagine life without Vittorio but couldn't.

Looking at him now talk with his grandmother, remembering the way he held Joe, as well as the way he made love to her, she wondered how she could have ever thought him dangerous. Wondered how she could have doubted his integrity.

Vitt suddenly looked up, caught her gaze, and smiled a slow, intensely physical smile that made her grow hot and cold. He was so incredibly sexual. He did things to her that she couldn't imagine any other man doing. And she liked how Vitt took her, possessed her, making her feel as if she really, truly belonged with him.

As if she were really, truly his woman.

As if she really, truly had a place here.

And she did want to belong to him, as well as belong here. It'd been years since she'd had a place to call home, much less a stable family.

Hours later when they were finally alone in their bedroom, Vittorio locked the door and dimmed the lights and Jillian smiled shyly. "You read my mind," she said, moving toward him and unzipping her dress as she walked.

He'd been unfastening the buttons on his shirt but his hands stilled as her dress slid to her hips and then she stepped out of it.

Her pulse drummed as she unhooked her black lace bra and then dropped it on the floor next to her cocktail dress. She felt Vitt's heavy-lidded gaze focus on her full, bare breasts, and her nipples tightened, puckering, and then his gaze dropped lower as she peeled off her black silk panties.

The air felt cool on her naked body and for a moment she wanted to cover herself but she didn't. Instead she held her ground and stood before him in just her black high heels and the emerald choker. She let him look, let him get his fill, before she slowly approached him.

His dark eyes burned her as she pushed him backward to sit on the edge of the bed. Her hands shook as she finished unbuttoning his shirt and pushed the soft cotton fabric over his shoulders and down his arms. As she freed his arms he reached out, palmed one of her breasts. Jillian shivered with pleasure, her legs like jelly.

She'd meant to be the one seducing him. She'd meant to show him she could give him the same pleasure he gave her, but Vittorio caught her in his arms, and rolled her onto her back and kissed her deeply, thoroughly. It was the way he used to kiss her before she'd run away from him, before she'd hid the pregnancy from him, before everything had become so awful.

She loved the kiss. She loved him. "Vittorio," she whispered against his mouth, burying her hands in his thick dark hair. He felt so good. He felt like everything she wanted and needed.

He pulled away to remove his trousers and then once naked, he stretched out over her, kissing her again, and then lower on her neck, and then down to her breasts where his tongue bathed and flicked one taut nipple, then the other.

He reached down between her thighs, discovered she was wet and then used his damp fingers to caress her, playing with the sensitive nub until she squirmed against his hand.

"You are always so greedy," he murmured in amusement as he stroked her again, apparently enjoying how her body shuddered and jerked against his.

"It's greedy to want you?"

"It's greedy to rush me," he answered.

"I can't help it. I just want you. Not an orgasm. Just you."

"That I can do."

She closed her eyes as his powerful thighs pushed her legs open wider. His erection was long and heavy and she felt it brush against her, and then Vittorio was entering her, stretching her to accommodate him.

She loved this moment when they became one, loved the feeling of possession and connection. So much of her life she felt alone, but when they were together like this, she felt whole and peaceful.

He slowly began to move in her and her hands stroked the length of his back, his skin warm and satin smooth beneath her palms. His body was hard and lean, beautifully muscled and she relished the width of his back, the smallness of his waist, the leanness of his hips and the small strong muscles in his butt.

She ran her hands over his butt, feeling the muscles tighten with each thrust of his powerful hips even as she pressed her mouth to his chest, his neck and his jaw. He smelled so good. He felt even better. *I love you,* she thought, as his hard strong body pushed her to the pinnacle of pleasure. *I will love you forever.*

CHAPTER ELEVEN

THEY'D made love again during the night and Jillian woke early the next morning still wrapped in Vittorio's arms.

It was the most amazing feeling in the world to wake in his arms. The most amazing thing to feel so safe. So loved. Because in his arms, against his warm chest, she felt loved. She felt perfect.

This was perfect. He was perfect. They could make this work, they could.

Turning in Vitt's arms, she pressed her cheek to his firm chest, her thighs brushing his. Closing her eyes she listened to the steady beat of his heart. She loved listening to his heart. It made everything simple and real. He was a man. She was a woman. And they fit together.

"What are you thinking about, *cara*?" Vitt's deep voice asked, rumbling through her.

"You. Me. Us. Everything."

"All without coffee?" he teased, lifting a hand to stroke her hair.

"Mmm." She smiled, snuggled closer, sliding one of her bare legs between his. "I loved last night. Thank you."

"My family was delighted to meet you too."

She giggled against him. "You know that's not what I mean. I was referring to us. Making love. It felt really good. It felt like it used to."

Vittorio continued to slowly, lazily stroke her hair, his hand running from the top of her head all the way down to her back. "It was good."

She felt like a cat beneath his caress and she arched a little with the pleasure. "I did like meeting your family though. And I adored your grandmother, as well as your father. You look so much like your father. Do you hear that often?"

"I do," Vitt agreed.

She pictured his father and the wheelchair with the ventilator tucked beneath. "Where was he shot?"

"He took a bullet in the back. Well, five actually, but the one that severed his spinal column was the one that nearly killed him." He paused. "Thank God it didn't. But he was in and out of hospitals for the next two years. Sometimes he still gets very sick."

She struggled to process what he'd told her. "But who actually shot him?"

"A member of the *cosca*," he said, using the Italian word for a Mafia clan or association. "As I told you last night, he wanted out. I was seventeen, the age many men join the brotherhood, but he made it clear that I wouldn't, nor would any of my children."

"I didn't think you could just walk away."

"You can't."

She heard the pain in his voice and moved closer. "What happened?"

He tensed. "My father announced he'd no longer be part of any criminal activity. He made it clear he would no longer extort money or provide kickbacks." Vittorio paused, stared up at the ceiling, deep lines etched next to his mouth. "We were all at dinner one night in Catania. My father and mother, my grandparents, my uncles, their wives, a few cousins and me. They called all the men out of the restaurant. My father knew what would happen. After all, he'd been a member for

years, just as my grandfather had been. He told everyone t
stay put, that he alone would go out. My grandfather and uncl
refused to let him go alone.

"They shot them all," Vitt said bluntly. "My father threv
himself over Giovanni, his younger brother, to shield hir
but it didn't matter. One of the bullets that struck my fathe
passed through him and killed Giovanni instantly. My fathe
alone survived. It's a miracle he did."

"And then your family was finally free?" she asked, he
voice husky with emotion.

"There was a huge public outcry. Everyone knew us ir
Catania. Everyone knew what had been done. People wer
livid. Even members of the association were uncomfortabl
with what happened. I think the taking of two lives, and th
maiming of my father, satisfied the clan's need to make a state
ment. Enough blood had been shed. We were left alone."

She pushed up on her elbow to look down on Vittorio.

"Your father saved you."

He swallowed roughly. "He did."

His face was etched in such hard lines of pain that it made
her heart ache. Gently she kissed his jaw, and his chin, and
then his mouth. "I wish your father was my father. He's such
a brave man."

Vitt reached for her, drew her up onto his chest and kissec
her back. "But he is your father now, and you are part of this
family now. We are one. You must believe that."

They kissed and then made love slowly, leisurely before
falling back asleep for another hour. But finally they rose and
showered together before collecting Joe from the nursery to
take him to have breakfast with them.

They were in the middle of having breakfast when Theresa
appeared, dressed in tailored cream slacks and a gold knit tank
with a rope of crystals, pearls and small gold beads around
her neck. She looked polished, wealthy and very angry.

"You had a phone call, Jillian," Theresa said shortly, "on the house phone. I wasn't about to chase you down so I took the number. You're to call him back. He said soon."

She handed Jillian a piece of paper. "It's not anyone working on the wedding. I know, because I asked him. Who else did you give our number to?"

Jillian shook her head. "No one."

"Must have been someone, because he called." Theresa smiled but even that was chilly. "Oh, and he's American. Apparently a friend with an urgent problem. Do call him back, but in the future, I'd prefer it if your friends used your wireless number."

Jillian felt Vitt's gaze and she turned to him. "I can't imagine who'd call."

"Go find out," he said, unconcerned. "Joe and I will be here waiting."

Jillian was troubled as she dialed the number Theresa had written down. She couldn't imagine who would call her at the d'Severano's Paterno castle. No one knew she was here. No one could possibly have the d'Severanos' number.

The phone rang three times before a man answered. "Hello?" he said.

"This is Jillian d'Severano returning your call. Whom am I speaking with?"

"A friend."

Her skin suddenly crawled. "My friends have names. What is yours?"

"Does it matter?"

"Yes, it does."

"In that case you can call me Mark, or Marco, whichever you prefer."

Jillian's legs nearly went out beneath her. Marco was the name of Katie's boyfriend. "Marco, you say?"

"That's what your sister called me."

She sank down on the white slipcovered couch in the sitting room. Her head spun. She felt close to fainting. "How... how... did you find me?"

"I have friends in high places. Police. CIA. FBI." He laughed a little. "Heck, I might even be a friend in a high place. I guess you never know, which is why it's important to know who your friends are."

"What do you want?"

"I'm sure you know what I want. It's what I—we—have always wanted. It's not very much. A few numbers. One little street address. And you're done."

"I'm sorry, I don't follow."

"I want your father's address."

"I don't know it."

He snorted. "You expect me to believe that?"

"It's the truth."

"But you could get it for me."

"I couldn't. He doesn't share it with me. I don't see him. I have no contact with him—"

"Those are excuses. I'm not interested in excuses. None of us are. What you need to do is think out of the box. Get creative. Invite him to your wedding. I am sure he'd be delighted by a trip to Italy if you asked him nicely."

Jillian's stomach rose, acid filled her throat. Marco knew too much. He was far too connected. Which made her wonder how he'd traced her here. "My father and I haven't talked in years."

"That's a shame, because you have so much at stake. Your baby...your husband...your new family."

She bent over, nauseated. "Don't threaten me."

"Then don't be stupid. You know what happened to Katie."

Briefly she closed her eyes, remembering Katie's violent death, remembering her own grief. Jill couldn't lose anyone else. Her heart couldn't bear the pain. "I would need time," she said, her voice low and broken.

"You don't have time. And you're not to involve your husband. He's not part of this. He's not to know about this. And should he find out, trust me, there will be *devastating consequences*."

Then he hung up.

Jillian slowly, numbly set the phone down and sat frozen on the edge of the couch.

For the past twenty months she'd been afraid of Vitt, terrified of his mafia connections, but Vitt wasn't a threat. He'd never been a threat. The threat was her family. The threat was her father's past. His choices. His actions. *Her* father was the danger. And as long as her father was alive, he'd always put the rest of them in danger.

But Jillian knew she could never turn on her father. Could never sell him out.

Something else would have to happen.

Something else would have to change to keep Vittorio and her baby safe.

Jillian returned to the breakfast room, but Vittorio was gone, just Theresa and Joe remained.

"Where's Vitt?" Jillian asked, scooping Joe up from his high chair.

"I don't know. He left the breakfast room not long after you did."

Jillian kissed Joe. "We'll go find him then," she said, struggling to keep her voice natural, to make everything seem normal. "See what he has planned for the day."

Theresa tipped her head back to look at Jillian. "This friend who called…he's not an old boyfriend, is he?"

"No." Again Jillian's stomach rose in protest. "Absolutely not."

"Who was he, then?"

"An acquaintance of my sister's. Just calling to check in."

"On our house phone?"

"He'd heard about the wedding."

"So he was calling to congratulate you?"

Jillian felt swamped by grief. "Yes."

"How good of him."

"Yes."

"Well, as long as that's the truth. Because you know Vittorio. He can't abide dishonesty." Then Theresa pushed back her chair, rose from the table and patted Joe's back before walking out.

For a moment after Theresa left Jillian couldn't move. She stood in the middle of the breakfast room, absolutely shell-shocked. Although sunshine still poured through the tall windows, splashing light across the tiled floor, Jillian couldn't focus. Couldn't see.

In less than five minutes Marco had turned her world inside out. In less than five minutes Marco had stripped away her security, and her hope.

Jillian wasn't sure her legs would hold her as she carried Joe up the stairs from the breakfast room to the nursery on the third floor.

Her heart thudded. Her teeth chattered. Her mind raced, thoughts spinning wildly in every direction.

What would she do now?

What could she do?

She had no idea how Marco had found her. But he had. And now that he had, she put everyone here in danger.

Like Katie before her, Marco's people would use her, make her a tool for destruction.

But she couldn't risk Vittorio's family's safety. And there was no way she'd ever hurt Vitt.

Not when she loved him. Not when he was the one person who'd reached out to her, helped her, loved her.

Because in her heart, she did feel loved. In her heart, she knew he'd do anything for her.

But she needed Vitt alive and strong for Joe. Because Joe, as a d'Severano, would need guidance. Joe would need the wisdom and courage of his father.

Drawing Joe closer against her breast, she breathed him in, smelling his sweetness, aware of his softness. She would never put her baby in danger. She would never compromise his safety in any way.

There was only one thing she could do.

Only one decision to be made.

She had to go. It was the only way.

Tears filmed her eyes and she blinked to clear her vision as she reached the top step. Joe stared into her face with concern and patted her cheek. "Mama," he said, his baby hand against her face, "Mama."

"It's okay," she soothed him, kissing his small palm. "Daddy loves you. Momma loves you. Everyone loves you."

Entering the nursery, Jillian found Maria folding Joe's clothes. At first glance, Jillian thought Maria must have done his laundry, but then she realized Maria was putting everything of Joe's into a suitcase.

Had Vittorio found out about Marco's call?

Was Vittorio sending them away?

"What are you doing?" Jillian asked Maria.

"Signor told me to pack the baby's things."

Jillian's legs shook. "Why?"

"He said that you were going on a trip."

"Me?"

Maria nodded, and Joe impatiently kicked, wanting to be put down. Numbly Jillian set him on his feet and just like the first day he was here, he raced toward his toys, pulling out a stuffed floppy dog off the bookshelf to squeeze to his chest.

Jillian drew a shallow breath. "When did he say that?"

"Five minutes ago. Maybe ten. He came into the nursery and told me to pack because the three of you were going away on holiday for a few days. Going to Capri, I think he said."

Relief coursed through her veins. "Capri?" Jillian repeated.

Maria folded another one of Joe's little T-shirts and added it to the stack in the suitcase. "He wants you to relax before the wedding. It's a pre-honeymoon honeymoon."

A pre-honeymoon honeymoon, to Capri no less. Vitt's thoughtfulness staggered her, aware that he knew it was one of the places she'd always wanted to go but had not yet been.

Shaking her head, Jillian looked off, across the bright nursery with its cheerful colors and fanciful fish. She loved this nursery almost as much as Joe did. It was such a perfect room for a little boy to call his own. "Maria, can I leave Joe here with you while I go talk to Signor?"

Maria smiled. "Of course."

Jillian left the nursery and headed down the hall for the bedroom she shared with Vitt.

The room was dimly lit as the curtains had been drawn against the morning sun. In the darkened room the large canopy bed looked massive and the antique wardrobe in the corner appeared to almost topple over. A suitcase lay open on the bed and Vitt's clothes were stacked in a neat pile in half of it.

Inside the bedroom she heard the sound of running water coming from the ensuite bathroom. Vitt was showering. Humming.

He sounded so happy.

It was such a small thing, but somehow it stole her breath, and practically brought her to her knees.

She couldn't hurt him. She couldn't do it. But just being here with him put everyone at risk.

And then the sound of running water stopped. Vitt had finished his shower.

Jillian put a hand to her middle. For a moment she felt so physically sick she thought she'd lose her breakfast right there on the elegant green-and-cream rug. But she couldn't afford to get sick. She had to keep herself together, had to talk to Vitt.

Gritting her teeth against the acid rising up in her throat, she opened the door and entered the bathroom.

Vitt was standing at the far end of the white marble room, naked, hard muscles glistening, with just a white towel wrapped neatly around his lean hips.

The long mirror over the double sinks was cloudy with steam and steam still wafted from the large white marble shower.

Vitt reached for another towel and began drying his thick hair. "How's your friend?" he asked, rubbing the towel over his wet hair.

"Good."

"Everything okay?"

She looked at him, knew she loved him, knew she'd do anything for him, just as she'd do anything for Joe. They were her family. They were hers to cherish. "Yes."

Vitt grinned as he dragged the towel over the back of his head. "Mother was worrying he was an old boyfriend."

Vitt's boyish grin nearly broke her heart. Jillian forced a smile. "She was wrong."

"I told her that."

Jillian exhaled hard. "It was an old friend of Katie's actually. He'd heard about the wedding. Wanted to offer his congratulations."

"Did you invite him?"

"No."

"Why not? He's welcome to attend."

Jillian turned away, close to throwing up. She couldn't do this. Couldn't pretend everything was fine when her heart was breaking. "He's not someone I'm close to." She ran a shaky hand through her hair, pushing it back from her face. "Maria's packing Joe's things. She said you're taking us to Capri for a few days."

Vitt draped the damp towel he'd used on his hair on a towel bar. "You weren't supposed to know," he said.

She stared at his broad, muscular back, his skin lightly golden, loving him more now, in this moment, than she'd ever loved him. "I'm still surprised. And delighted. We're really going to Capri?"

"Yes." He turned, glanced at her in the mirror, his dark eyes locking with hers. "You said you'd never been."

"You remembered."

"I remember everything."

Hot tears pricked her eyes but she wouldn't cry. Not now. Not when she had to be strong. "Thank you."

"The trip sounds all right?"

"Heavenly," she said, meaning it, because all she wanted was to be with Vittorio. All she wanted was time with him. To make love with him. To have a life with him. "When do we leave?"

"Soon. I've a quick meeting in Catania, and then my driver will bring you and Joe to meet me at the airport. We'll fly out at noon. Can you manage that?"

"Easily. What should I pack for the trip?"

"Nothing. I'm buying you a new wardrobe there."

"You're serious?"

"Your clothes are horrendous. And you are absolutely gorgeous and I can't have my beautiful bride running around in mom-wear...even if she is the mother of my son."

Her heart ached, and she swallowed around the lump filling her throat. "I don't need that much. A few pretty dresses, yes, maybe a wrap to cover a new swimsuit, but I don't need more than that, not when I have you."

His dark gaze met hers in the mirror again. "You really are happy with me?"

"Yes."

"You don't feel as if I've forced you into this?"

"No." She felt like she was dying on the inside. Her heart seemed to be coming apart, twisting, writhing, bursting into little bits of nothing. "So I'll pack a few things and then see you at the airport."

"In ninety minutes. My driver will be waiting downstairs for you. As soon as you're ready, jump in the car." He walked toward her, dropped a kiss on her lips, stroked her cheek and then again, smiling into her eyes. "Green eyes," he murmured. "I love them."

"Thank you."

"You're going to love Capri."

She rose up on tiptoe to brush her mouth against his. His warm mouth sent a tingle down her back. "I know I will if you're there."

"See you soon," he said.

"See you soon," she answered, grateful she had the acting skills to hide the fact that her heart was breaking.

After Vittorio dressed and left, Jillian packed the few things she had into the battered green suitcase, an old suitcase that reminded her of a bruised avocado. As she packed, she tried not to think about what she was doing, or what was happening, or where she'd be going. Because she wasn't going to Capri and she wouldn't be meeting Vittorio.

Instead she was using the opportunity to leave Vittorio.

And she'd be leaving Joe here with Vitt.

Her insides writhed with pain at the idea of it, so she jammed her emotions down, suppressing them with all her strength.

She wasn't going to think right now. She wasn't going to feel. She was just going to put one foot in front of the other and do what she had to.

Suitcase packed, she carried it to the top of the stairs, knowing that Maria and Joe were waiting for her by the front door. But before she headed down, she went to the nursery, peeked inside for one last time.

This is it, she thought, glancing around, trying to remember all the details. The color blue. The painted fish. The crisp white bookshelves.

This is where Joe would sleep at night, safe, secure, protected.

This is where he'd grow up, adored, loved.

It was good that she was leaving him here. It was good he'd be raised by such a strong, moral, compassionate father.

Now all she had to do was go. Her bag was packed. The car was waiting. The only thing remaining was to walk out the door, and close it, and leave her husband and baby behind.

Imagining walking away from Joe made her knees buckle. She put out a hand, touched the wall, took a deep shuddering breath.

You can do this, she told herself. *You have to.*

Joe was too innocent and beautiful for the life she'd lived these past fourteen years. Joe was too innocent to be caught up in her family's darkness and turmoil.

With a last glance around the bright cheerful nursery, she saw how the warm sunlight shone through the windows and fell onto the crib. The light was good. The warmth even better. Leaving Joe here was the right thing to do.

Jillian went down the stairs to the front door where Maria was waiting with Joe and the luggage. The lump in her throat was beyond horrendous. It was murder to swallow and her eyes felt scalded but she would not let the tears fall.

Vittorio would be angry. He'd be so furious that she'd left

them. But she hoped one day he'd understand. She hoped one day he'd realize she was doing this to protect them, not hurt them.

"I've one last thing to do," Jillian told Maria, her voice cracking. "Can you take the baby for a quick walk around the terrace? Let him touch the roses. He loves the flowers. And then he and I will go."

Jill didn't kiss Joe, or make a sound, as Maria carried Joe out, because God knew, she couldn't leave if Joe started crying. But Joe didn't cry. He was happy to go outside, loved the pretty roses, and as Maria carried him, he looked over Maria's shoulder and smiled at his mother, waving, *bye-bye*.

Bye-bye.

Bye-bye, my love. Bye-bye, my baby. For a split second Jillian nearly screamed with the pain. She couldn't do this. She couldn't. There was no way…

And then she lifted her hand and smiled and waved back to her boy. Bye-bye, my heart.

And as the door to the terrace closed behind Maria, Jillian picked up her own suitcase, leaving Joe's two small bags on the gleaming floor, and headed out the front door to climb into the car.

Vittorio wrapped up his meeting early and headed straight for the executive airport, anxious to see Jillian and Joe and be on their way for their three-day holiday. But on reaching the airport in Catania, he discovered his driver hadn't arrived yet.

He waited ten minutes then called his driver. His driver immediately answered. "How far away are you?" Vitt asked, glancing at his watch.

"I've just returned to Paterno," his driver said. "I dropped Signore off at the airport."

"But I'm at the airport. I've been here. The jet's fueled and waiting."

"Signore said I was to take her to the public airport."

"What?"

"She said there had been a change of plans."

A change of plans? Why would there be a change of plans? Vittorio reeled from shock and struggled to speak. "Where is my son?"

"Here in Paterno, at home."

Thank God. Vittorio exhaled. "But the Signore?"

"She is gone."

Vittorio immediately jumped into his car and drove home, unable to believe that Jillian had really gone.

As he drove through the gates of his estate, he played his last conversation with Jillian over and over in his head. She'd said she was looking forward to Capri. Said she was happy with him.

So why would she leave?

In the house, he dropped keys on the ornate sideboard in the hall next to the vase of fresh flowers and stood frozen in place.

How could everything have changed so quickly? Just hours ago everything had seemed so perfect he'd planned an impromptu getaway to his favorite five-star hotel in Capri. But just hours later, Jillian was gone and she'd abandoned him, abandoned their son.

Why?

How?

Something must have happened. Something must have driven her away. But what? Or more accurately, who?

He replayed the morning's events over in his head one more time, picturing waking up with her, making love, showering, breakfast, his mother's appearance...

The phone call.

The phone call.

Someone had said something to her. Scared her. Threatened her. Chased her off.

He'd find out who called the house. There were ways to trace numbers. Even unlisted numbers.

He climbed the stairs to the library, determined to find out everything he could when he heard the sound of his father's wheelchair down the hall.

Vitt paused at the top of the stairs and spotted his father waiting for him at the door of the library. But his father wasn't the only one in the wheelchair. Eleven-month-old Joseph lay on his grandfather's chest, his thumb in his mouth, sound asleep.

"Where has she gone?" Salvatore asked Vittorio.

"I don't know."

"Why would she leave her son?"

"I don't know that, either."

His father stared at him hard. "Has she done this before?"

"Never."

"Then why now?" his father demanded.

"I don't know. But trust me, I'm going to find out."

Jillian had purchased a last-minute seat on an Air Italia flight from Catania to Heathrow. From Heathrow she'd catch the cheapest flight she could to the States. Where in the States she didn't know. She'd figure that part out later. It was hard enough just leaving Vittorio and Joe behind in Sicily without thinking of the vast Atlantic Ocean separating them.

The flight attendant on Air Italia offered Jillian snacks and drinks but Jillian shook her head, unable to speak, almost catatonic with despair.

What had she done? How could she have left them both? Why hadn't she gone straight to Vittorio and told him everything?

Because you're scared, a little voice whispered. You're scared that if you make a mistake, you could lose the people you love.

And she did love Vitt, just as she loved Joe. She loved them so much she wanted to be brave and strong and do what Salvatore had done—sacrifice herself for the good of his family, but how it hurt. It hurt so bad she wasn't sure she could survive it.

Arriving in Heathrow, Jillian purchased the cheapest ticket she could on a U.S. airline, which ended up being to Houston, Texas.

She didn't want to go to Houston. But she didn't know where else to go. The problem was, she didn't want to go to the States. She wanted to jump back on a plane for Catania. She wanted to tell Vittorio she couldn't live without him and yet she was so afraid of him being hurt. For the two hours before her flight, Jillian wandered around the international terminal in a fog.

Nothing about leaving Paterno felt right.

Nothing about leaving Joe and Vittorio felt right.

But what else could she do?

What else should she have done?

She should have talked to Vitt. She should have trusted him, because somewhere inside of her she knew he could handle the very real things she was afraid of. Look at his father. Look at what he'd gone through in his own life. He wasn't a man who crumbled in the face of adversity. He was a man who met it head on. Fierce. Tough. Unflinching.

Instead she'd tried to handle everything on her own, the way she had for the past fourteen years.

But her way didn't work. Her way meant she was lonely. Her way meant leaving everyone she loved behind.

There had to be a better way. Because this way was hell. It was madness.

It was breaking her heart.

She'd had enough of heartbreak and madness. She'd suffered through far too much pain.

If only she could reach Vitt. If only she could call him before it was too late. He might be angry but she thought perhaps he'd understand. Perhaps he'd realize she was trying to do the right thing, trying to be strong, trying to be independent, which in this case, seemed to be absolutely wrong.

If only she knew how to trust better. If only she could trust him...

And then it hit her. She did.

Jillian raced to find a bank of phones, but there weren't many in the airport, not with so many people carrying their own phones now. Finally she found a cluster of phones, but as she picked up the receiver she realized she didn't even know Vittorio's number, nor did she have a number for his family.

What about his office in Catania? Surely that would be listed. She called information and gave him the d'Severano name, asking if they had any businesses by that listing. They did not. And then she ran out of ideas, because she didn't know the name of his company.

Just as she hadn't taken the time to really know Vitt.

There was so much she'd do differently given the chance. So much she wanted to know, so many things she wanted to do with him.

Travel, explore, talk, make love.

Have more kids.

An announcement sounded through the terminal that Continental Airlines was now boarding their afternoon flight to Houston.

Heart in her mouth, she watched the other passengers line up at the gate. She watched all two hundred passengers board, but her legs wouldn't move. She couldn't line up. Couldn't do it.

The gate personnel were finished boarding but they didn't close the door. Instead the gate agent paged her. "Jillian Smith, this is your final call. Jillian Smith, your final call for Continental Airlines Flight 52."

Jillian glanced down at the boarding pass crumpled in her damp hand, and then at the gate agent, and realized that even though her initial reaction was to leave her family to protect them, she knew it was the wrong one.

Family didn't leave family.

Family didn't betray family.

Family protected family.

And Jillian needed hers.

It struck her that she didn't have to run anymore. She didn't have to be afraid. She had Vittorio. He was smart. He was strong. And he could be trusted.

Eyes burning, throat aching, she picked up her small carry-on bag and turned her back on fear, and walked through the terminal, past security, out the airport terminal to the curb.

It was twilight and the sky was lavender and gray. Jillian stood on the curb trying to figure out how she'd get back to Catania and what she'd say to Vitt once she got there when a deep voice spoke behind her.

"Thinking of going somewhere?"

Vittorio.

Usually deep and calm, his voice sounded rough and as if he was in pain.

She turned to face the man who'd turned her life upside down in the best way possible. He looked tall and handsome and worried. He looked so very dear. It didn't hurt that he had a small boy in his arms that meant everything to her.

"Yes," she said, tears filling her eyes as she looked at the two people she loved most in the world. "I want to go home."

For fourteen years she'd had to take care of herself. For

ourteen years she'd had to pretend she didn't need anything from anyone, when in truth, she needed everything.

Love, comfort, tenderness, support.

"I want to go home with you. Please take me back to Paterno," she choked.

The haunted expression lifted from Vittorio's dark eyes and then he slowly smiled. "I hoped you'd say that."

"Oh, Vitt, I don't know what I'm doing. I just know that I got scared, but I'm so tired of being scared, Vitt. I'm so tired of running and looking over my shoulder and worrying the bad guys will find me."

"I guess one found you this morning," Vitt said, wrapping his free arm around her, bringing her close to him.

"Yes." She pressed her cheek to his chest, feeling the warmth of her husband and son. "But I should have come to you, Vitt. I should have told you. You wouldn't have panicked. You would have known what to do."

"Marco can't hurt you," Vitt answered, brushing his lips across her brow as his arm squeezed tighter around her waist. "The FBI were able to trace his call. It came from near a cell tower in downtown Detroit and the Detroit police arrested him an hour ago. The police have been looking for him since your sister's death, and now they have him. He's going away for a long time. He won't ever be able to threaten you again."

Jillian's lips curved in a watery smile. "So you did know what to do."

"I'm a d'Severano, *cara*. I know how to take care of my family."

His deep voice rumbled through her, his tone fierce, proud. "Am I still your family?"

"Forever."

Tears filled her eyes. Her chest grew tight and she struggled to take a breath. "I'm sorry I didn't trust you. I'm sorry I didn't

come to you right away. I was just so scared he'd hurt you o:
Joe or someone else in your family—"

Vitt reached up to wipe her tears away. "I understand. Jus
as I understand you've had no one to be there for you since
you were a little girl. But we'll work on trust, and we'll lear
to be a strong family together, yes?"

"Yes." She blinked to clear her vision. "So you're not ma⟨
at me?"

"Of course not."

Joe wiggled in Vittorio's arms, and reached out with bot⟨
arms to Jillian. "Mama."

Jillian looked up, over Joe's head, to Vitt. "Can I hold
him?"

"You better. Your little boy cried for you endlessly or
the plane. Fortunately it was my own plane so no one com-
plained."

Jillian didn't know whether to laugh or cry. And then
she laughed because Vittorio had the most amazing way o⟨
making her feel good. With him, life was the way she'd always
dreamed it should be.

"Can we go home now?" she asked.

"Most definitely."

EPILOGUE

ELEVEN-and-a-half-month-old Joseph was supposed to be the ring boy, but he refused to walk down the aisle in his miniature black suit to the front of the d'Severano chapel where Vitt waited in his elegant black tuxedo. Instead Joseph walked down the aisle swinging his pillow in circles before stopping at his grandfather's wheelchair at the outside of the wooden pews.

"Up," he said to Salvatore, dropping his pillow. "Up, Papa," he repeated, wanting to be put on his grandfather's lap, because in his nine days in Paterno he'd learned to love many things and many people but his grandfather Salvatore was probably his favorite.

His grandmother Theresa put a hand on Joseph's shoulder and tried to steer her grandson toward the front of the chapel, but Joseph squawked in protest.

Checking his smile, Vitt stepped down from the stone steps before the altar and placed his son on his father's lap.

"Vittorio," his mother said softly, reprovingly, slim and chic as ever in a pale silvery-gray fitted gown.

Vitt shrugged. "It's his day, too. He should sit where he wants, and if he wants his grandfather, who am I to say no?"

Salvatore smiled at Vitt and then down at Joseph as the little boy squirmed to get closer to Salvatore's chest.

Vittorio clapped his father on the shoulder and then returned to the front of the church as the string quartet played the first bright notes by Vivaldi.

Jillian appeared in the arched doors at the back of the chapel. The ends of the pews were decorated with flowers. The old stone chapel glowed with candlelight. Guests crowded the pews but Jillian only had eyes for Vittorio who looked impossibly handsome in his black tux and white dress shirt with the white tie.

Hers, she thought, on a quick breath. He was hers. And she knew he'd always be hers.

Her lover. Her partner. Her husband.

She walked down the aisle on her own, her ivory gown rustling, her legs shaking with every step, yet knowing that once she reached the front of the chapel she'd never be alone again. She'd have Vittorio. She'd have his family. They'd be a family.

Reaching the front of the chapel, Vitt stepped forward to take her hand. His beautiful face looked somber in the candlelight but then he smiled and love raced through her, love, desire and joy.

The ceremony passed in a blur, with Jillian seeing nothing but Vittorio's beautiful face and dark eyes. They said their vows, exchanged rings, kissed as her heart turned over.

She was home.

She finally belonged somewhere.

And then the ceremony was over and she was walking with Vittorio down the aisle. The chapel smelled of gardenias and orange blossoms and the soft candlelight reflected off the arched ceiling and the high stone walls. Faces smiled at them as they passed the crowded pews, but then they were alone in the small antechamber. It was dark and blissfully cool.

Vittorio dropped his head, kissed her and kissed her again.

"I love you," he said as the chapel bells pealed high overhead.

"Even though your family was shocked when you told them who I was yesterday?"

"They're fine. They're used to drama," he answered with a grin. "I don't know what we'd do without some excitement."

Jillian tried to smile but tears filled her eyes. "You're too good to me."

"Impossible. You deserve so much happiness."

"You've made me happier than I ever dreamed I could be."

"Good. I'm glad." He tipped her chin up so he could look into her eyes. "I have loved you since you walked through the lobby of the Ciragan Palace in your black management suit with your midheight heels. You were the picture of efficiency and yet somehow you stole my heart. I'd never thought about settling down and then suddenly all I wanted was to marry you and take care of you forever, and I mean that Jill Anne Carol Lee, I do."

She sniffed and laughed, her fragrant bouquet crushed between them. "You can just call me Jill. It's shorter."

"Not Alessia?"

Jillian shuddered. "Never Alessia. She's gone. Dead. But oh, I do like being your Jill. I like it more than anything."

He smoothed her crisp white veil back from her face and then caressed one of her dark red curls that rested on her bare collarbone. "And I love your green eyes and your red hair and your infamous family history," he said, before glancing over his shoulder, aware that any moment the doors would open and family and friends would pour out. "I love everything about you."

Jillian laughed and lifted her lips for him to kiss her, and then kiss her again. "Good," she murmured against his lips, "because you've got me now."

"Finally." He gazed down at her, his dark eyes holding hers for an endless moment before he whispered in Sicilian *"T'amu bidduzza." I love you, beautiful.*

Eyes stinging, heart overflowing, she reached up, touched Vitt's lean bronzed cheek, dazzled by joy. "I can't believe it."

"Believe what?"

"I've come home." Her voice broke, her expression one of wonder. "I've finally come home, haven't I?"

"You have," he answered, dropping his head to kiss her deeply, even as the chapel doors burst open and their family and friends surged out to celebrate their love.

Harlequin Presents

Coming Next Month

from **Harlequin Presents® EXTRA**. Available August 9, 2011

#161 REPUTATION IN TATTERS
Maggie Cox
Rescued by the Rich Man

#162 THE IMPOVERISHED PRINCESS
Robyn Donald
Rescued by the Rich Man

#163 THE MAN SHE LOVES TO HATE
Kelly Hunter
Dirty Filthy Money

#164 THE PRIVILEGED AND THE DAMNED
Kimberly Lang
Dirty Filthy Money

Coming Next Month

from **Harlequin Presents®**. Available August 30, 2011

#3011 BRIDE FOR REAL
Lynne Graham
The Volakis Vow

#3012 THE STOLEN BRIDE
Abby Green
The Notorious Wolfes

#3013 TOO PROUD TO BE BOUGHT
Sharon Kendrick

#3014 FROM DIRT TO DIAMONDS
Julia James

#3015 THE SECRET BABY SCANDAL
Jennie Lucas & Kate Hewitt

#3016 MARRIAGE MADE ON PAPER
Maisey Yates

Visit www.HarlequinInsideRomance.com
for more information on upcoming titles!

New York Times *and* USA TODAY *bestselling author
Maya Banks presents a brand-new miniseries*

PREGNANCY & PASSION

*When four irresistible tycoons face
the consequences of temptation.*

Book 1—ENTICED BY HIS FORGOTTEN LOVER

Available September 2011 from Harlequin® Desire®!

Rafael de Luca had been in bad situations before. A crowded ballroom could never make him sweat.

These people would never know that he had no memory of any of them.

He surveyed the party with grim tolerance, searching for the source of his unease.

At first his gaze flickered past her, but he yanked his attention back to a woman across the room. Her stare bored holes through him. Unflinching and steady, even when his eyes locked with hers.

Petite, even in heels, she had a creamy olive complexion. A wealth of inky-black curls cascaded over her shoulders and her eyes were equally dark.

She looked at him as if she'd already judged him and found him lacking. He'd never seen her before in his life. Or had he?

He cursed the gaping hole in his memory. He'd been diagnosed with selective amnesia after his accident four months ago. Which seemed like complete and utter bull. No one got amnesia except hysterical women in bad soap operas.

With a smile, he disengaged himself from the group

around him and made his way to the mystery woman.

She wasn't coy. She stared straight at him as he approached, her chin thrust upward in defiance.

"Excuse me, but have we met?" he asked in his smoothest voice.

His gaze moved over the generous swell of her breasts pushed up by the empire waist of her black cocktail dress.

When he glanced back up at her face, he saw fury in her eyes.

"Have we *met?*" Her voice was barely a whisper, but he felt each word like the crack of a whip.

Before he could process her response, she nailed him with a right hook. He stumbled back, holding his nose.

One of his guards stepped between Rafe and the woman, accidentally sending her to one knee. Her hand flew to the folds of her dress.

It was then, as she cupped her belly, that the realization hit him. She was pregnant.

Her eyes flashing, she turned and ran down the marble hallway.

Rafael ran after her. He burst from the hotel lobby, and saw two shoes sparkling in the moonlight, twinkling at him.

He blew out his breath in frustration and then shoved the pair of sparkly, ultrafeminine heels at his head of security.

"Find the woman who wore these shoes."

Will Rafael find his mystery woman?
Find out in Maya Banks's passionate new novel
ENTICED BY HIS FORGOTTEN LOVER
Available September 2011 from Harlequin® Desire®!

HDEXP0911

Harlequin® *Desire*

ALWAYS POWERFUL, PASSIONATE AND PROVOCATIVE.

**NEW YORK TIMES AND USA TODAY
BESTSELLING AUTHOR**

MAYA BANKS

**BRINGS YOU THE FIRST STORY
IN A BRAND-NEW MINISERIES**

PASSION & PREGNANCY
*When irresistible tycoons
face the consequences of temptation.*

ENTICED BY HIS
FORGOTTEN LOVER

A bout of amnesia…a mysterious woman
he can't resist…a pregnancy shocker.

When Rafael de Luca's memory comes
crashing back, it will change everything.

*Available September
wherever books are sold.*

Harlequin

SuperRomance

Love and family secrets collide in
a powerful new trilogy from

Linda Warren

the Hardin Boys

Blood is thicker than oil

Coming August 9, 2011.

The Texan's Secret

Before Chance Hardin can join his brothers in
their new oil business, he must reveal a secret
that could tear their family apart. And his
desire for family has never been stronger, all
because of beautiful Shay Dumont.
A woman with a secret of her own....

The Texan's Bride
(October 11, 2011)

The Texan's Christmas
(December 6, 2011)

HSR71723